Crudo

Also by Olivia Laing

To the River

The Trip to Echo Spring

The Lonely City

OLIVIA LAING

Crudo

PICADOR

First published 2018 by Picador
an imprint of Pan Macmillan
20 New Wharf Road, London N1 9RR
Associated companies throughout the world
www.panmacmillan.com

ISBN 978-1-5098-9283-9

1 3 5 7 9 8 6 4 2

A CIP catalogue record for this book is available from the British Library.

Printed and bound by CPI Group (UK) Ltd, Croydon, CR0 4YY

Visit www.picador.com to read more about all our books
and to buy them. You will also find features, author interviews and
news of any author events, and you can sign up for e-newsletters
so that you're always first to hear about our new releases.

For Ian, of course
and for Kathy

A complete list of quoted material can be found
at the back of this book.

The cheap 12 inch sq. marble tiles behind speaker at UN always bothered me. I will replace with beautiful large marble slabs if they ask me.

Contents

ANYWAY

1

KNOTS

34

SWIMMING IN THE AIR

67

NOT YOU

83

PAPERS & PAINTS

115

ANYWAY

Kathy, by which I mean I, was getting married. Kathy, by which I mean I, had just got off a plane from New York. It was 19:45 on 13 May 2017. She'd been upgraded to business, she was feeling fancy, she bought two bottles of duty-free champagne in orange boxes, that was the kind of person she was going to be from now on. Kathy was met at the airport by the man she was living with, soon to become the man she was going to marry, soon, presumably, to become the man she had married and so on till death. In the car, the man told her that he had eaten dinner with the man she, Kathy, was sleeping with, along with a woman they both knew. They had also been drinking champagne, he told her. They laughed a lot. Kathy stopped speaking. This was the point at which her life took an abrupt turn, though in fact the man with whom she was sleeping would not break up with her for another five days, on headed writing paper. He didn't think two writers should be together. Kathy had written several books – *Great Expectations*, *Blood and Guts in High School*, I expect you've heard of them. The man with whom she was sleeping had not written any books. Kathy was angry. I mean I. I was angry. And then I got married.

Two and a half months later, pre-wedding, post-decision to wed, Kathy found herself in Italy. She had been interviewed at the Register Office, she had not known her husband's date of birth but nobody thought she, or he, were being trafficked. They were civil, they had chosen their songs, she'd insisted on Maria Callas because she didn't operate via understatement. Now, 2 August 2017, she was sitting under a hornets' nest in the Val d'Orcia. She could have sat in several other places but she'd become fond of the hornets. Yesterday, two of them had fallen on her leg, still fucking. It was a good omen, her friend Joseph said when she emailed him about it.

She had a good routine going. First she swam twenty lengths, that woke her up. Then she drank coffee, then she arranged a sunlounger under the hornet tree. At ten she made her husband bring her more coffee. She hadn't had a husband before but she knew how it worked. Was Kathy nice? Unclear. Kathy was interested in her tan, she was interested in Twitter, she was interested in seeing whether any of her friends were having a better holiday than her. Beside her, her husband was peeling off wet swimming trunks under a green towel. Everything was nicer than at home. Not a little bit nicer, but profoundly, like every material had been reinvented by a smarter species. Kathy and her husband had accidentally gone on holiday with the super-rich.

They didn't pass, obviously. They weren't even trying. They ate their potato foam penitently, they spilled passata and plum-cardamom gelato down every T-shirt they owned. There was a laundry service but they were alarmed at the cost. Maybe they could wear darker clothes, or find a laundry in Rome.

It was the brightest day imaginable. Something weird had happened to the sky, it wasn't clear or cloudy but somewhere in between. The light wasn't concentrated in the sun, it was everywhere at once, like being inside a halogen bulb. Kathy had a headache. The internet was excited because the President had just sacked someone. Got hired, divorced, had a baby, and fired in ten days. Like a fruit fly, some joker wrote. 56,152 likes. None of it was funny, or maybe it all was.

Kathy had no parents, which didn't stop them annoying her. She thought about them a lot. Her mother had committed suicide, her father had vanished before she was even born. She was an orphan, truly Dickensian. Her husband actually called her Pip, sometimes the Pip. He was a very nice man, indisputably nice, everyone liked him, it was impossible not to. I always felt we were friends outside the poetry circle, his friend Paul Buck wrote, congratulating them on the wedding that still hadn't quite happened and continuing with an anecdote about how he and Kathy had failed to have sex once.

It was getting hotter and hotter. 31 degrees, 36 degrees, 38 degrees. There were wildfires across Europe. One of them had been started by someone throwing a cigarette butt out of a car. Kathy stood neck-deep in the pool and thought about nothing. Wants go so deep there is no way of getting them out of the body, she'd written in the final paragraph of her last book. Her ear had become blocked by water and every hour or so it cleared for a moment and then quickly something rose up inside it like a thick wad of chewing gum, like a sock. It was unpleasant, the sense of something pressing at her interior, it dragged her down. In the bar her husband read a list of the hotel chef's celebrity clients. Who's Rachael Ray, he said, who's Gloria Estefan, who's Peyton Manning? She didn't know who Peyton Manning was but she helped him with the rest.

Here's what they ate. They ate porchetta in rolls and porchetta on rocket. They ate a kind of yoghurt cream dusted with lavender and tiny meringues. They ate rack of lamb and black cod and picci with pork ragù. They were definitely getting fatter. Have you noticed, she asked him, how everyone has younger wives here? It was like the second-wife club. Personally she was a third wife, so on that level at least she fitted right in.

What Kathy wanted currently was complicated to explain. She wanted three or four houses so that she could move between them. She was happiest on her travels, like a clockwork toy, maybe happiest unpacking or booking a train ticket. She liked to get in and settle down and she also liked to snap shut the door. She wanted to write another book, obviously, and she wanted to find a way of situating it nowhere. Nowhere like the interior spaces of the body, nowhere like the dead zones of a city. She was a New Yorker, she wasn't meant to be in Europe, she certainly didn't belong in a damp garden in England. The weeds were alarming, she was terrified of moths and mould. What she really liked was lizards, not just their tiny dashing feet but the way they were exceptionally dry. Kathy liked dryness, she'd always been the supplicant but now that she'd finally got things settled she was finding an abnormal talent for withholding, as if she'd finally become one of the many men she'd chased across Berlin, London, San Diego. In the 1990s, when she was young, she'd wept and sliced up her own flesh at the blink of an eye, she loved to get truly abject, but now she'd dried out, she was as cool and brown and flat as a piece of discarded toast, not appetising exactly, not desirable, but fodder for someone, a pigeon at least.

Was this getting older? Kathy was worried about ageing, she hadn't realised youth wasn't a permanent state, that she wouldn't always be cute and hopeless and forgivable. She wasn't stupid, she was just greedy: she wanted it always to be the first time. When she thought about the people she'd populated her youth with she cringed. She could have made it so much more glamorous, so much more debonair, she needn't have had a bowl cut, she needn't have worn dungarees, the minutes were passing, she'd failed to get a death-grip on time. Now she was cool, but old; now she was hot, but wrinkled. My life is delicate (more delicate than my cunt), she'd written to a boyfriend not that long ago. I've had eleven abortions, she told someone else, which wasn't even true. Kathy was always lying, she'd lied since she was a small child with unattractive red hair. When her hair began to fall out because of the stress of living with her mother she told the girls at school that it had been eaten by her rabbit. At that school they had

a playground game where everyone tried to ꭐ
themselves and then lift someone's body with just t..
little fingers. The girl about to be lifted had to lie flat
and everyone had to press on her as hard as they could.
After that the lifting was easy. Weightlessness was
another exclusive possession of the very young. Later
on you started clanking around like tins tied to a car.

What Kathy was supposed to be doing was planning
her wedding. She did this by looking through pictures
on Instagram and making unkind comments. That's
very vulgar, she or her husband would say. Chairs and
tables, napkins, that's very vulgar. At this rate they'd end
up getting married in a car park.

Kathy loved her husband. Last night they'd been
forced to give a reading together, which wasn't exactly
her bag, and yet she'd found herself pleased to hear
his poems, like someone wiggling a key in the lock of
language, it's jammed, it's jammed, and then abruptly
stepping through. For some reason there were three
psychiatrists at the reading, one apparently very eminent and two from Sheffield, still in their swimsuits. A
patrician man sat at the back and called out questions.
There's hope for us all, he said, inexplicably. At dinner
that night Kathy found herself sitting next to him.
Felicia, Felicia, he said, this is the writer. Felicia had the

7

ly posh. Kathy recoiled into her
ny white sliver, and waited for the

t's going to be 41 degrees, her husband
06 in Fahrenheit. So when people in India
an   ulf States have temperatures of 50 that's very
hot. No wonder they're dying. Pretty much 30 degrees
above normal blood temperature. He was wearing a
pink T-shirt and his left leg, which he'd burned earlier
in the week, had begun to peel. A drill had started up
somewhere. Kathy was writing everything down in her
notebook, and had become abruptly anxious that she
might exhaust the present and find herself out at the
front, alone on the crest of time – absurd, but sometimes don't you think we can't all be moving through
it together, the whole green simultaneity of life, like
sharks abruptly revealed in a breaking wave? Possibly
her speeding thoughts presaged a migraine, possibly. On
Twitter a Chinese photographer had gone missing.
She'd last been seen at the funeral of her husband, who
had won the Nobel Peace Prize and then spent the rest
of his life in prison. Kathy had seen a photo of her,
tightly wound in sunglasses. Anyway, she'd gone. And
there'd been a statement from the government that had
stuck in her mind, something about discarding the ashes

in the sea, was that right. When the accusations about Jimmy Savile reached a pitch of plausibility his gravestone had been taken up in the night and ground into gravel and used to resurface roads. This too didn't sound quite right but that's how Kathy remembered it. The Jimmy Savile dust could be anywhere by now, sticking to car tyres and inching relentlessly off the island, no doubt especially on ferries. Evil was a subject of interest for Kathy, she wasn't squeamish, she'd worked years in a strip joint in Times Square, she knew about appetite and dead eyes. She used to do a Santa Claus routine, anything not to be bored, releasing her flat little fried-egg tits into the eyes of the world. Nobody knew anything about life who hadn't breathed a good lug of that pissy, spunky air, oh Kathy'd really seen it all. I want to know why a president is always a john and never a hooker, Zoe Leonard once wrote in a famous much-reproduced poem and Kathy felt like it was still a good question now, why some people always bought and never sold.

She was forty. She'd had breast cancer twice, she'd barely ever not had some kind of STD, she spent more time in the GUM clinic than her own front room. She'd owned several apartments in several countries, selling and buying, trying to take advantage of shifts in the market, mostly failing. People took her photograph often, she'd ditched the old look, her head wasn't shaved now, she was a true bottle-blonde. She had a thrift-shop Chanel suit hanging in her room, far too hot for that here, dumb to put it in her case even, though she had hopes for Rome. Is it hot in Rome she asked her husband and he replied with a grunt. So maybe the suit was a waste of space, so what. Tomorrow they were supposed to be going to dinner with a famous opera singer, right here in the Tuscan hills. The patrician man came past, slapping in his sandals. Not a bad life, he said. *Insparring.* He was hosting a toga party that night and was concerned about noise. Kathy had recently complained to the owner of the hotel about a drone some guests had been flying above her sun-lounger. She didn't like being watched and she didn't like the sound, which at first she'd mistaken for an especially agitated bee. The owner agreed with her, he had many famous guests, names you'd know immediately, and he didn't think drones had a place here. It struck Kathy now that she too was a kind of drone and that perhaps what she was doing, writing everyone down in her little book, wasn't exactly gracious. Then again she liked the idea of herself up in the air with her compound eyes, hovering, havering, gathering data.

There used to be bombing raids right here, her husband had told her. He was an expert on bombing but he had not, he said, known that the Americans had bombed civilians in Italy. I was surprised that the Americans had been so assiduous about bombing and strafing civilians, he said. And children. It was a fact that a great deal of people had been killed right here, of many different nationalities and political allegiances, partisans soldiers prisoners of war farmers refugees the starving people who walked from Rome and Siena and sat at the gates, waiting for food. A few days back there had been a wedding at the hotel, and Kathy had sat with a lunch-time beer and watched some florists from Florence assembling a complicated half-arch out of pink roses. Also watching was an elderly man whose father had been shot dead right there in the square, in the last year of the war. There was a plaque about it, which later the bride stood under for her official photograph. That was history, that was how it went, now they were tearing out all the 1970s ceilings and making it look medieval again, only with rainfall showers. It was hopeless, it was crazy, just the mess that time made. A little white road through the valley, that was the ground, but you could draw pretty much anything on top, bodies or children with tubas or a Ferrari being towed by a pick-up.

At lunch, more pork, the patrician man and his wife were at the next table. Again, he leant over. Where are you getting married, he said. Kathy didn't know how he knew she was getting married and frankly she wasn't thrilled about it. Dick, she muttered under her breath. His name was Henry, she didn't even need to ask, she could just tell. Henry chuntered for a while about shadow Labour ministers being thick as shit. She turned down the peerage Felicia said. I'm not surprised, she'd been passed over twice. Kathy liked proximity to people with information, she wouldn't have been a good spy, it all went through her, like a sieve. She just wanted to nibble on it for a minute. Henry was handsome. He looked like an untrustworthy fox in a Disney film. A very short fat man came into the bar and greeted everyone by name.

While Kathy was watching the preparations for the wedding she'd absolutely and completely forgotten she was about to have one of her own. She'd actually already purchased the dress, Isabel Marant, too short, no surprises there. Some people she knew, friends really, had expressed surprise and doubt that Kathy would be willing to share the spotlight for long enough to actually make her vows. She'd once physically pushed another writer off the stage and she had a lot of subtler moves too.

Lots of things happened that night, 3 August 2017. For example Kathy met a major donor to the Democratic Party. As it happened this was the second major donor to the Democratic Party she'd met in two days. They know Hillary really well, someone told her. The donor had an extraordinary daughter called Dahlia, who was the most poised person Kathy had ever met. She was wearing a clinging dress that had been crocheted in several strong colours, blue and yellow and black, and she looked terrific, really lovely. She was nineteen, maybe twenty, and she ran the conversation like a world-class tennis player, serving generously, returning every ball. Nice she said fondly when an adult nervously volunteered information about their home life or occupation. Nice. Next! She told Kathy about what politics meant and also what engineering meant and the differing but similar ways in which they could change the world. Her mother leaned in to volunteer that she too was writing a book, though it was going quite slowly what with living between LA, Tuscany and Israel and having several houses and working in the film business and giving up a year to volunteer for Hillary.

What Kathy really wanted was for them to Dish about the victory night non-party, but that wasn't happening. The conversation moved on to kosher food. At my brother's bar mitzvah, Dahlia told Kathy, the hotel wouldn't serve cake after meat. And we were like it's a party and they were like it's a kosher hotel. We got round it though. We got them to serve it at midnight. Yeah, we had to have cake.

After this Kathy got into a ding-dong with an artist, a sculptor in leather sandals who had at some point in the evening cut his leg. Blood was pouring down his ankle, but nobody else seemed to have noticed, so Kathy kept quiet. They argued about Wordsworth and Europe. Kathy had really quite passionate feelings about what he was saying and why it was wrong. The rosé had got into her and made her snappy. She felt strongly and with conviction that British people had always hated Europeans. Like Anne Boleyn. Nobody liked that Frenchified bitch. She was also certain that the Field of the Cloth of Gold was central to her arguments though to be honest she couldn't actually remember its purpose or participants. Anyway, her husband leant over the table and said not even very gently you are completely wrong, and since he genuinely did know everything she was quite happy to relinquish the argument and move on to another one, about publishing. Here she was on much stronger ground, though by now the alcohol had kicked in and everyone began repeating themselves and drawing irrational conclusions.

They left early. They were meant to go to a serious dinner but her husband had begun to complain tragically and with feeling about a nausea he believed related to the lunchtime pork so in the end they didn't attend, which made them both feel like absolute crumbs. Kathy didn't sleep. She moved beds twice. A hornet was stuck on the inside of the insect screen. The air conditioning was revolving the air in the room without actually cooling it. In the morning her husband woke up and said I dreamt every time I rolled over I had to give you a little disintegrating box. It was hot, it was perfect, it was nearly right now.

*

Breakfast. Three triangles of watermelon, one cup of coffee, one pot of yoghurt, one small jar of honey. That's how it went. Other people ate strawberry crostata or wholemeal croissants or heaven forbid eggs five ways and a selection of meats. The toga people were emerging, hungover and victorious. Hello Harry, hello Lordy. I woke up and I've got a stye. Bloody painful.

No I've never had one, how have I bloody well got one today. They had conducted their festivities in a tent on the terrace. It was still there now, empty and doleful, poles festooned with ivy and small pale flowers. They were talking about the tower block that had burned down. I was coming along the Westway and there it was, all blackened said the stye woman. How many people died, eighty, eighty-five. But they don't know yet. Fire that hot you don't get bodies. What about bones. I think they do it by the teeth. Kathy's husband pushed several grapes into his mouth at once. He was listening to a different conversation, between a guest and an Italian lawyer. I was brought up Catholic, Opus Dei, I know what it's like, the lawyer said. Mafia, the guest said and the lawyer shrugged hugely.

On a sunlounger a few minutes later, Kathy assessed her life choices. Not bad. She was forty, she had a small diamond on her right hand, she was looking at a mountain, no one currently was in her way. She was completely alone, but utterly surrounded. Last night, before going out, she'd had a serious conversation with her husband about marriage. I don't like proximity, she told him. But why he kept saying. What's the source of that feeling. It wasn't a feeling that had a source, except in the way the source of hay fever is flowers. It was just she kept sneezing, it was just that she needed seven hours weeks months years a day totally alone, trawling the bottom of the ocean, it's why she spent so much time on the internet. So you like talking but you don't like it when people talk back her husband said rudely, but that wasn't quite it. She just didn't know how to deal with someone else being there, especially asleep. She was right on the edge of the bed, she was doing her best. In two weeks she'd make official promises, in language as embarrassingly hewn and potentially hubristic as the Labour manifesto Ed Miliband had had carved into stone. Where was that stone, she wondered. Had it too been turned into tarmac? Were all the roads in England composed of memorials that had become publicly toxic? She looked on the internet. The EdStone was in the garden of the Ivy. I promise to control immigration, I promise homes to buy and actions on rent, with this NHS I commit to time to care, I wed a country where the next generation has higher living standards than the last. How long did they think it could go on for. Kathy wanted the NHS forever obviously, but she was fairly certain that by the time she was an old lady they'd be eating out of rubbish dumps, sheltering from a broiling impossible sun. It was all done, it was over, there wasn't any hope. The week before she left Britain an iceberg the size of Delaware broke off the Larsen C ice shelf and floated away. The Gulf of Mexico was full of dead fish, there was a trash heap circulating in the ocean that would take a week to walk across. She tried to limit her husband's addiction to the tumble dryer, she never flew to anywhere more than eight hours away, but even lying here on her back she was probably despoiling something. What a waste, what a crime, to wreck a world so abundantly full of different kinds of flowers. Kathy hated it, living at the end of the world, but then she couldn't help but find it interesting, watching people herself included compulsively foul their nest.

Because she'd dreamt about him, Kathy had emailed her previous lover. She kept it light, she wanted him to know she was having a good time. Hot in Tuscany she said sunnily. Come see us when you're back. Last time she'd seen him was in the bar of a cinema. She'd drunk beer, he'd drunk coffee. I have to go he said, I'm having tea with the King of Spain. She was suspicious but when she got home she Googled and the King of Spain was definitely in town. That had been several weeks ago, and her email was only two sentences long but nevertheless her ex responded as if she'd been ceaselessly badgering him for the past three months. He expressed ignorance about her region of Italy, concern about the wildfires and then told her he would see her in the autumn. Disappearing now, he concluded. Kathy had made a career an entire life an art out of continual disappearances and she was incensed at being upstaged. I'm IN ANOTHER COUNTRY she shouted to her husband. I HAVE ALREADY DISAPPEARED. Why does he always try and OUT-DISAPPEAR ME. She really was angry. Why are you so feverish about Sébastien, her husband asked reasonably. She tried to explain, it wasn't that she missed him exactly, or that she liked him exactly, more that she felt continually outmanoeuvred. She'd once made a film with a man with whom she was/wasn't having an affair. It was called *Blue Tape*. She had been a paragon of invincibility she hadn't given a half a quarter an eighth of an inch. She'd had all the cards, she sucked the man's cock while he stuttered and stumbled and then she directed him through a passable hand job, not like that, not like that, faster, higher, more precise. At the end he was a wreck and she sat on the couch composed and triumphant, that she thought now was a successful relationship.

Power and ice, their similarities. Maybe her edges were melting, maybe she was being subsumed, maybe she should grow up, maybe this is what adulthood was supposed to be like, a glacier toppling into a bath. Why do you need to win everything Kathy, why do you think it's such a fucking race. She had gone to a very exclusive private school, she was always a little smelly, she was the cleverest girl bar two. Who were twins, imagine, with extremely wealthy blonde hair. The place sucked, the place blew, she wanted to be the absolute best especially since nobody liked her or even talked to her much, but the twins the twins were extraordinarily talented and naturally gifted, also they had that multi-lingual good manners veneer that only comes with money. Kathy's family was rich too but in a more chaotic withholding way, like actually her grandmother held the purse-strings and her mother was pretty much a hobo, a Barneys and the Plaza wreck, she went to the sort of stores where French boys would purse their lips and say non, disgusting to the first outfit and aiaiai madame to the second, no matter what it looked like. Her mother bought it, she always bought it, this was the 1980s, she bought it Every Single Time. It's Alaïa Kathy, it's Comme Kathy, it's a white cowl with bat sleeves Kathy, I'm wearing it to lunch. Later Kathy would take it from her closet and wear it to school, chew the sleeves in maths class, get an A but not the best A, consider her future. This wasn't exactly the future she'd considered, but after the Times Square years she knew it could be a whole lot worse.

What had happened to her mother is that she'd cut her wrists in the bathtub. What had happened to her mother is that she had checked into a slightly rundown once quite exclusive still pretty nice hotel, tipped the bellboy, chatted to the night staff and then OD'd in the bedroom, not paying the bill. Kathy had spent maybe two days maybe two weeks hysterical, calling all the hospitals, trying to track her down before the rest of the family thought to tell her. They were that kind of family, estranged, huge upholstered couches of absolute silence between them. When her grandmother died a few years later, of natural causes, Kathy thought she would inherit a fairly substantial whack; indeed many people thought she had inherited a fairly substantial whack but that was quite wrong. She lived off hustle and her books and she got by, but the days of being wealthy though behind and all about her were not in fact ongoing.

Her husband leant over at that moment and said did you hear those people at breakfast? They said where's David? David's in his room looking for his passport and money. Every time he stays in a hotel he hides them in a different secret place and then he can never find them again. I'm putting the tickets at the back of my red notebook, her husband continued. I want you to know that. He'd spent the entire morning at reception, attempting to buy their train tickets to Rome. It had been quite successful in the end, it had necessitated several phone calls in multiple languages, he held the printout proudly.

The afternoon went slightly downhill. They ate and then waited under the hornet tree for their bags to be moved from their third room to their fourth. The third room had been quite ordinary, just a regular apartment, but in the fourth they were restored to the pinnacle of luxury. The room was constructed like a New York loft that had been placed under exposed Tuscan beams and roof tiles. The bathroom was enormous and had a glass door. I confess I was rather unsure about that too her husband said when she pointed it out. Kathy fell asleep and woke to what she thought was thunder but was apparently more bags on the move. She picked up her laptop and leafed through the internet. Almost imme-diately two things annoyed her. One was an article about a painter she liked by a critic she hated. The other was a profile in an American magazine about a novelist. What especially annoyed her was a comparison between the novelist's latest book and an oral history of

Chernobyl. But her imaginary oral histories are exquisitely attuned to the ways in which humans victimise each other, it said. Kathy's least favourite word on earth was exquisite. Kathy found nuclear war a considerably more seemly subject than nuclear families. Kathy was avant-garde, middle-class-in-flight, Kathy did not like the bourgeoisie. It was too fucking hot, she had better things to do than read about the window frames in other people's houses. She lay on her back and stared at the tiles. What, exactly?

Her husband had begun a soliloquy about Oat Krunchies. They were little bits of oats like a pillow with air in the middle so when you bit on them they went crunch and collapsed. They weren't very nice, not really. Oh go away you stupid thing. Britain indeed. Sorry, it was just pointing at something on Twitter I didn't like. Well now I have a photo of your extended neck, that's nice. She loved it when he began to ramble. Sometimes she'd catch him at home doing a complicated task, maybe baking bread or making a sauce and speaking to himself in a low confiding tone, offering exhortation and encouragement, like a small boy only not at all ridiculous. If this was love she'd take it, lying next to him naked, both fiddling with their phones. Earlier, he'd ordered ice cream in an Italian accent and couldn't believe it when she told him he was speaking English. He could speak Italian, he'd just gone off on the wrong foot.

Everyone had a husband here. She'd never spent much time with heterosexuals, she didn't know there were so many of them, and all so similar. White people, men older, women younger. She'd met one woman in the bar, made eye contact, possibly said hi and the woman had seized upon her and began to speak unceasingly, as if she was being interviewed for a documentary exclusively about her life and times. She told Kathy about her daughter's school, her son's school, she told her about her tiny little house in Sloane Square and her estate in Warwickshire, so nice, she articulated clearly, for the children to have room to run around. She bemoaned parents who hired tutors for their children and then she described her son's tutor quite a different kind of tutor, who had advised them to let him be exactly as he was. She looked like a little doll, like a little pleased girl with well-brushed hair, it seemed impossible that she might be a mother, but there they were, her children, drifting into disaffected view. Kathy had the same shoes as the daughter but in a different colour, it was embarrassing, it didn't make a bond. She had so clear a sense of light coming through an oak tree that afterwards she thought the woman had described it, but no, it was just the emoji the visual read her brain pulled up when someone said Warwickshire. The woman's husband was called Boris, he'd quit his job, sometimes Kathy saw him around on the way to the pool and she'd bob one finger and smile. Rich heterosexuals, landed, entitled, when she said husband she didn't mean that.

★

It hadn't always been like this. In New York in the spring, Kathy had stayed in a railroad apartment in Bushwick. There were no doors between the rooms, and before she went to sleep each night she unknotted two strips of indigo fabric to screen off the bedroom from the kitchen. The light still leaked through, but the real obstacle to sleep was the small grey cat, the apartment's permanent official resident. It was a street cat with skinny flanks and a bobtail like a rabbit. From the beginning the cat took against her. It expressed its displeasure by crying and smashing glasses, and eating the invitation to the Comme des Garçons press preview at the Met. One night it put its front paws into its water bowl and smashed it repeatedly into the kitchen cupboard. It's not like Kathy was doing much of anything, except meeting friends and talking feverishly, but she still wanted to sleep at night. This went on for five days. It threw up on the rug, it kicked granules of piss-soaked litter all over the floor and then walked them into her sheets, it covered her clothes and laptop in fur and dust. Was it sick? Its coat had lost its sheen, its flanks were hollow, it woke her at 2 and 2:30 and 3 until she was so tired she walked into walls and trapped her finger bloodily in the shower stall. Everything was dirty, mould in the grout, grease around the cooker, New York dirt, no big deal, just eight generations of people living in the same small rooms. The wardrobe key jammed and Kathy had to take the door off its hinges with a kitchen knife, then the front key snapped off in the lock as she was coming home. Bodies: hers wasn't feeling good. Everyone was in town for Frieze, she kept running into Matt, she saw Charlie and Rich. She saw people she hadn't seen in years, London people, art world people like Tom and Nicky. It felt like all the doors were open and she could pass into practically any room, she was so happy and so tired, a crop of spots by her mouth, drinking too much coffee, getting caught in a storm on 1st Avenue, running up the street jumping puddles in rain so hard it took her shoes two days to dry. In the end the owner of the flat arranged for a friend to take care of the cat. All Kathy had to do was deliver it in a cab. She assembled its arsenal of possessions, its litter tray and litter and biscuits and bowls. She tucked a chewed toy mouse in and looked around for the cat. It was sleeping on a shelf. She climbed up on a stool and lifted it down, claws flailing. In the cab it vomited noisily in its carrier and then howled with despair. Crawling across the Williamsburg Bridge in pouring rain, the driver kept talking about his friend's pitbull while she wanted to weep with misery for the cat's unhappiness, its soiled state. When she got back she scrubbed the floors and took all the bedding to the laundry and that night she slept on clean sheets like a Kushner, like a king.

Everyone was there, it was a village, it was truly great. Kathy went for eggs with Sarah, Matt came in, they walked together to Abraco to find David. Charlie was at the Standard with Paul, you're all talking British the other Matt said. Joseph was early, it was his early stage, he kept beating her everywhere. 3pm, he texted. Read it and weep. Is New York different, people kept asking, do you feel like it's changed. She hadn't been back for a year, the longest spell she'd ever spent away. It was the week Obamacare was rolled back, everyone was talking about pre-existing conditions. David was wearing a ski jacket zipped to the neck. I don't even have a body, I'm so fat. David and Kathy had once spent an afternoon discussing how they'd kill themselves in elaborate detail in a borrowed apartment on 46th Street. They were both so unhappy then, it was like a touchstone to know there was a way to stop it. But here they still were. The line of stubble along his jaw was white, he still walked on tippy-toes like a little boy. There were white hairs in Kathy's bangs too, a white stripe. She cut her own hair in the bathroom, she took out the trash.

She was walking down 1st Avenue when the Comey news broke. 9 May 2017, early evening. Carl texted, Twitter's ABLAZE gurl. Everyone was saying it was a banana republic, at dinner Jim said what blows my mind is that we'll be talking about this in years to come, what we were doing, but we'll know how it panned out. They ate Chicken Zsa Zsa and salad, they ate foie gras, they drank beer and Riesling, they laughed all night, that was the night the President fired the Director of the FBI, they were scared and sick, Jim said he's taking a giant shit on our nation. It wasn't quite warm, earlier she'd bought mint ice cream from a bodega and the Chinese guy behind the counter hadn't understood the word plasters, you mean Band-Aid? Her feet were bleeding from new trainers, new Nikes she'd bought in Barneys that afternoon. The weather was never hot enough, though when Marc lovely Marc said it was the most beautiful spring he'd ever seen she'd agreed, it was, it was so green and excessive, so floral and bosomy and bedecked. Everyone talked about politics all the time but no one knew what was happening. This is what it's like in dictatorships, Alex said, people only know what's happening because of gossip. Alex was Russian, his grandfather had been Stalin's chief bodyguard, he knew what he was talking about Kathy figured. This was 40, she'd thought in her little bed over Ireland, upgraded as previously mentioned, this was the whole fucking trip.

★

It was their penultimate day in Italy. 5 August 2017. Her husband had been on the terrace, he relayed a conversation with the eminent psychiatrist. I only give second opinions, he'd said. I work on a knife-edge, I have to get it right. The people I see are wealthy, auto-cratic, psychotic, used to complete control – oh look there's the lizard. Her husband loved lizards. This one was green, like an elegant crocodile, its legs moved like someone riding a bicycle. Periodically it stopped, lifted its head and sniffed the air. Now it was looking back over its shoulder, exposing a paler belly. Her husband was rapt, he looked bewitched. I just love it he said. Whole minutes of lizard watching are so rare. It's coming back over here. What's he doing now, behind the tree trunk? Probably hiding back in the flower bed now, don't you think?

Kathy had always had unsatisfactory relationships and her current unsatisfactory relationship was with sleep. Sleep was a withholding lover. She lay there and waited for it, hot and itchy and uncertain. Was enough written about sleep. It was so delightful, the bit when you were just toppling over the edge. A butterfly with markings like piano keys came past. She'd been lying face down on her lounger, her cheek jammed into a damp towel. She wanted to drift off but instead she kept remembering troublesome things, like the paedophile who'd been moved into a house on her old road. She was going out with Sébastien at the time, it was him who'd found out about the paedophile and really it was him who'd kept her abreast as the case developed. At first it seemed that something small had been blown out of proportion but later like something big and seriously unpleasant had been hushed up, which is to say that the paedophile was still living happily or not in the same house and riding about Kathy's own streets on his bike, a little rumpled and sorrowful but very much at large. The last time Kathy had seen Sébastien he'd given her an update, I hadn't thought about it for weeks he'd said, but I knew I was seeing you so I looked it up. It made Kathy feel uneasy, that they'd been so linked in his mind, but then it had also made her uneasy when Sébastien used to lean against her window giving her larky reports on where he thought the paedophile might be. It occurred to her that she might have bad judgement about people. The problem, she knew, she'd actually written it down, was that she liked liars and evasive people, she liked seeing what they'd say, she liked being continually shocked surprised disappointed by the way they were never where she thought they'd be, it was the same exactly as how she felt watching a lizard vanish into a previously invisible crack or cranny, something in her applauded any instinct for freedom, however personally inconvenient to her. The paedophile however she wanted locked up, she was opposed to prisons in 99% of all cases the exception being this. She was for any expression of sexuality whatsoever, nothing shocked her except an absence of consent, not when there were a million at least people who wanted, who really got hot about acting out no consent, there was no need. Just images, some people she knew had said in the paedophile's defence, as if the small bodies depicted weren't real, somewhere, hurt.

She went to the pool and swam hard. There was quite a lot of grit in the corner by the steps. It was possible indeed likely that this was her fault, since she had been continually disobeying the rule about washing feet before entering the water, along with the rule about not swimming before 8 in the morning or after 7 at night. She swam when she liked, and at night she didn't bother with a swimsuit either. Fuck the rich, she waved her small white bottom like a flag against them.

It struck Kathy that she was not unevasive herself. Take her novels. She liked to steal other people's stories, just lift them wholesale. I am Toulouse Lautrec, I'm a totally hideous monster. I'm too ugly to go out into the world. I am Laure the schoolgirl, I thought you didn't notice me because I'm so invisible. I'm born poor St Helen's Isle of Wight. 1790. As a child I have hardly any food to eat. Behind her an Australian girl was on the phone to her mother. It's an eleventh-century village, it's not very baby-friendly, it's beautiful, no it's beautiful here. She had silver flatforms and Kathy hated her because the previous day she'd stolen her sun-lounger, literally just lifted her towel and books off it and dumped them on the ground. I read an article about how self-soothing is good for babies, I'm a bit worried Laura's going to believe in that shit. Yep she said eleven times. Exactly. Oh fuck, now she was talking about her breast enlargements. It should take four months for the swelling to go down, if in four months they're still too big for my liking I can have a one-night operation a very non-invasive procedure. We think we want to build a house rather than buy a house. What was she, twenty-four. We might fly to Mexico on 21 September. Well, nothing's set in stone. Jamaica, would you be okay with Jamaica? It was all the same thing, it was the world talking. You couldn't hate it, or you did but that was just more of the same, another opinionated little voice in an indecently augmented chorus.

KNOTS

Kathy did not have a happy time in Rome. It was too hot, the taxi driver's air conditioning had broken on Friday, it was now Sunday 6 August 2017, the taxi was its own ecosystem of damp woolly air. She and her husband lay naked on their hotel bed and panted. Then they went for a walk which accidentally transitioned into going to mass. Kathy hadn't been to mass since some time in the 1980s, she forgot to genuflect and then crossed herself with the wrong hand. There were two nuns in the front with lovely gauzy veils. The priest gave a sermon in Italian in which the word WhatsApp was frequently discernible. Kathy felt moved and then hot and then irritable and then absolutely claustro-phobic. They had a dinner reservation, she didn't have time for this. She got up and edged her way to the door. Children were gallivanting in the aisle, it wasn't like St Joseph's circa 1983.

In the restaurant Kathy and her husband had an enormous fight. It started because she put two of his prosciutto and fig ciabattas on her plate. He had four, they were enormous doughy pillows, the same unpleasant temperature as the room. Her husband was furious but Kathy's fury as ever was larger and less ambiguous. She maintained it at the same pitch for several hours, hissing and eye-rolling, the whole works. She had a vicious stomach ache, she might plausibly faint, there was a full moon but her husband couldn't even follow the bouncing blue dot on Google Maps, craning over his phone with his mouth hanging open. She hated him, she hated any kind of warmth or dependency, she wanted to take up residence as an ice cube in a long glass of aqua frizzante. Anyway they sorted it out, after she'd banished him to the lobby and sweated alone for 45 minutes, examining the world by way of her scrying glass, Twitter.

Now they were in the air, Italy like a cauliflower protruding beneath them, extending into a really blue luminous expanse of sea, a green hem by the beaches like boiled glass. A small white plane moved rapidly through a different shelf of air. At the airport Kathy had become a connoisseur of T-shirts. I Only like Positive People. Hello darling Happy Spring. The best T-shirt she'd ever seen was in the ready-meal aisle in Brighton Waitrose, well it ain't going to suck itself. A Brazilian boy had once come up to Kathy in there, hands shaking, whole body trembling, and asked if she'd sleep with him. She'd just swum round the ruins of the West Pier, she was giving off some kind of wild energy, a person who didn't give a fuck about personal safety or concealed dangers. She still remembered how it felt to reach open water, the way her body was tugged and slammed, the sense she'd had of a vast metal skeleton just below the surface, girders poking up like fork prongs. Beneath her the sea, beneath her a mountain range with its own armada of creamy cloud.

Sometimes I drag my lover into the shade of *sotoportego*, inside a dark *corte*, I steal a voluptuous embrace. Back home, back in England, Kathy was reading about Venice. She also read a humorous article about make up for vaginas and the beginning and end of an essay in the *London Review of Books* about young men escaping Mosul. I never saw such terrified people in my life as a group of young men who had run away from Mosul waiting to be vetted by Iraqi security to see if they were former IS fighters. Two men of military age went into a tent for questioning. They were carried to the camp hospital on stretchers two hours later covered in blood. There was currently, Kathy thought, a problem with putting things together. It had always been a problem but the blind spot had been bigger. Ten years ago, maybe even five, it was possible to ignore atrocities, to believe that these things happened somewhere else, in a different order of reality from your own. Now, perhaps because of the internet, it was like the blind spot had got very small, and motionful like a marble. You couldn't rely on it. You could go on holiday but you knew corpses washed up there, if not now then then, or later.

There is no away to throw things to, that was an environmental slogan Kathy had internalised several decades ago, which was why she was having to find homes for the several dozen almost empty bottles, tins and spray-cans of cleaning products she'd hoarded in her various cupboards, believing it was better if she did her share of custodianship rather than dumping every-thing in the landfill in which they'd all soon be living.

She was moving house, she was finally and unequivo-cally moving in with her husband. She'd been living for nearly a year now in his much larger substantially more desirable house, but she'd kept on her own, first because of her abnormal need for solitude/escape hatches, then because she had to have somewhere to fuck Sébastien. That's an expensive trick pad, Joseph had told her when she unpacked the whole thing for him on Avenue A. They were in a diner they liked called Yucca. Every time she returned to New York she walked down A in terror lest Yucca be shuttered. It was holding out for now, unlike Gracefully or French Roast or the willow outside the Avenue C version of 9th St Espresso. They sat outside always, once they'd been verbally attacked there by a Ukrainian witch, an event Joseph perpetually tried to spin into a blessing. Anyway it was a nice place, the huevos rancheros were notably yolky. And Joseph was right, it was an expensive trick pad and since the trick had flown it was time to do without it.

Kathy had removed all the things she actually liked and was surprised at how little attachment she now felt to what had been her cherished and longish-term home. She put things in a bag, she put the bag in the bin, she wheeled the bin outside the house. They weren't curable, she didn't need them, they were broken and hopeless. 6% of her possessions had already gone to one of three charity shops, she was purging and experiencing a little of the pure light-headed ecstasy she habitually felt after being violently sick. Saintly, even. Divested of mismatched socks, old bottles of nail varnish remover, bags of soda crystals someone else had abandoned. The soda crystals were unopened. She snatched them back and put them in the car.

A funny thing: she'd begun hearing voices. It had happened now three times in maybe six days, that she'd find she'd tuned into a frequency in which a human voice was whispering, just below the threshold of actual words, a sort of impassioned mumble, a communicative withholding tone. Eventually the line would sever. It had happened once when she was lying on her lounger with the breast augmentation woman behind her. That time the voice was incantatory and not a little malevolent; for a minute she genuinely thought the woman was cursing her, before she realised she was wearing earbuds that might plausibly be leaking. The next time, also in Italy, she'd distinctly heard her husband muttering something, which woke her abruptly up, only he wasn't in the room and indeed when questioned had been in the pool. Sometimes Kathy's mind ran too fast, it was very pleasurable and almost invariably was the prelude to a migraine. She wasn't worried about the voices. They were just the uninvited accompaniment to a change in her way of life, an auditory elevator between floors.

It rained substantially, it rained like something was being emptied from a bucket. Kathy packed up her house and ran back and forth to the car, carrying her possessions. The sky was green and flickering. Driving home, her husband told her that when he got his own flat in the 1990s, after the drawn-out end of his first marriage, he sat among the unopened boxes for days, feeling utterly miserable. Why, she asked, but he wasn't sure. The water was hitting the roof so hard it was ricocheting upwards, the air was full of water moving rapidly in many directions, causing small white explosions.

Kathy was ecstatic to be able to sleep alone again, she loved travelling through dreams in her big white bed. I'm born crazy in the Barbican, she writes in her notebook, propped on her duvet. I'm crazy as a bedbug. I could lead more of my double sexual life in SF etc. She dreams of huts, a tree which is the world which is her back.

The next morning the senior sales negotiator of an estate agent emails her. He offers her a flat on the Golden Lane estate in London, England. She looks at the photographs. The flat is a single room, in which there is a double bed, a yellow chair, possibly Eames, and a G-Plan sideboard. Reflected in the mirror is a small desk. From the bed she can see the Barbican, its distinctive upturned balconies. Its Brutalist architectural theme has now made the Golden Lane an icon in its own right, the email informs her, benefitting from simple designs, clean lines and wide windows. The estate was named after Golden Lane which dates back to the thirteenth century taking the name of a Street on the original site. There is a pink print of a shopping trolley on the wall. 30 square metres, terrazzo panelling and sliding doors. She considers buying it.

What Kathy would like is to escape herself. Abundant amounts of storage, direct access to four of London's International Airports. When she was anorexic in the aughts like everyone she was conducting an assault on gravity, she was the apple that would go upwards, that simple. How nice to astonish the philosophers, to go off like a firecracker in all their faces. She wishes her history would go away, leaving holes. There is no story, she writes, I'm going crazy. It's a cry.

*

It was beginning to seem like the world might be about to end. Enjoy August she read on a site she'd only opened to read a book review: conspiracy theorists say it might be your last month on Earth. Beneath it, in a column titled Most Popular, was a headline in red: Woman liveblogged her rape on Instagram. A New Yorker travelling in South Africa. She'd kissed the man and then shared a hot shower with him. It was almost an intuitive thing, she told *Marie Claire*. I was still in the bathroom – in the crime scene. I don't even think I'd stood up. I just typed and typed. The hashtags on her Instagram pictures included two iterations of her own name, along with africa, survivor, humanitarian and victimblaming. At one of Joseph's birthday parties there'd been an almost-fight about how many times people had been raped. I've been raped three times Gerry said and someone replied sweetly well you know what they say, three times a lady. The first time Kathy met Gerry, and in fact the second and third, she believed Gerry was a drag queen and kept calling her he. It was right at the beginning of pronouns, and she was a little irritated when Joseph kept correcting her. Eventually the truth dawned, though truly Gerry was a priestess and beyond gender, the oldest and most glitzy club kid in town.

What was more worrying was Trump and North Korea. People said nothing was going to happen, but since people by which she meant pundits had wholly and absolutely failed to predict any of the carnage of the past year, she doubted their reliability. She decided to look at his Twitter, to check it out. It was worse than she'd expected. He was retweeting Fox News about jets in Guam that could fight tonight, but he was also taking time out to trashtalk the FailingNewYorkTimes. My first order as President was to renovate and modernize our nuclear arsenal. It is now far stronger and more powerful than ever before . . . . . . Hopefully we will never have to use this power, but there will never be a time that we are not the most powerful nation in the world! When? When had he done that? She missed Obama. Everyone missed Obama. She missed the sense of time as something serious and diminishing, she didn't like living in the permanent present of the id.

If the world was about to end was there anything she should be doing? She was getting married in nine days, she was doing a studio visit for an artist who made fruitful annihilating porcelain sculptures out of bodies that were morphing into flowers and flowers that were morphing into bodies. She loved them, they looked like charnel pits and also decorations for expensive cakes, like synchronised swimmers in the pit of the damned. She might as well do that as anything else, she might as well have chicken for Lauren's birthday and file a review, she might as well continue with her small and cultivated life, pick the dahlias, stake the ones that had fallen down, she'd always known whatever it was wasn't going to last for long.

Kathy wasn't a conspiracy theorist, though Kathy was fairly paranoid she didn't like subscribing to anything, but all the same she was fairly sure someone was moving pieces somewhere out of view. Someone was getting rich on all this, she knew they were. Food insecurity, water insecurity, the collapse of the state, sick desperate people, it was an excellent way to make a buck, to make what Gary Indiana once described as the Freudian faecal pile. Anxious, uneasy, with a small persistent pain in her left knee, Kathy began to itemise the things that were sitting on her table, a blanket box that had previously belonged, like the room itself, to her husband's previous wife, a famous writer who had died the previous year. Flexitol heel balm, Comme des Garçons wallet, almost empty bottle of green mineral water from Sainsbury's. Moth trap, sunglasses, Pantone 7461 mug of pens, ten stones, an unattractive ring she'd bought in a car boot sale several maybe even ten years before. There were no moths in the moth trap, just one small fly. Would they die? They would most certainly die. There was also her phone, a prehistoric Nokia given to her by her friend Matt, and her diary, mustard-coloured, given to her by her half-sister, Wendy, who was a comedy agent, soon to be a partner, extremely high-flying. Burns, shock waves, radiation, that was how it went, then obviously other more secondary things like associated violence, or lack of food or some-thing quite random. Everything was so intricate, it was amazing how much of it sustained from day to day. The city panics, she writes. Bombers terrorists're going to take over! She writes down the worst things she can imagine, she puts herself in a small room and lets herself be raped and beaten, it doesn't lessen the anxiety, the world so blue, gone in a moment, up in smoke.

Maybe you're dying and you don't care anymore. You don't have anything more to say. In the nothingness, the gray, islands almost disappear into the water. She's writing down the plot of *Key Largo*, making it as depressing as she can, sketching out a landscape for the end of the world. Every piece of meat, every cunt. Is she getting repetitive? There were things you could do once that you can't do anymore, short skirts but in sentences-form. The reason she liked tattoos was that she liked something getting under her skin and staying there, it was pretty much the only experience of permanence she had. Oh Kathy, nobody wanted you. Oh Kathy, now they do.

*

10 August 2017. She arrives at her old house 4 seconds before the movers. Moving day, a neighbour she's never seen before shouts. I didn't know you were getting

married. Inside, she explains to a man called Alan that the kitchen door needs to be taken off its hinges to get the bed down the stairs. Then she unlocks her bike, unused for a year and covered in a thick smock of cobwebs, and walks away.

Everyone is out on the streets. A man called Stan in a straw hat and filthy suit is ahead of her in the queue for the post office. Another man walks in. Hello Malcolm X top of the morning hello Malcolm X top of the morning hello Malcolm X Malcolm XXX. She sends a parcel to Italy, chooses the second cheapest option. At home, their possessions have been covered in white sheets. Everyone drinks coffee. The curtains are down. It's August but it feels like autumn, slanting light, a smell of rot and ripeness. It's pleasant but makes her feel bad, like a lot of old news is churning under the surface, returning unexpectedly. Memory showers desire, desire infects memory. Upstairs, she reads the flight log of Capt. William 'Deak' Parsons, who dropped Little Boy on Hiroshima. 03:00 final loading of gun, 07:30 red plugs in, 08:38 leveled off at 32,700 feet, 09:15 ½ drop bomb. Then she reads about Oppenheimer, then she reads about Oppenheimer's daughter Toni. After his death she wanted to become a translator for the UN but she wasn't given security clearance on account of her father and so she killed herself at the age of 32.

A story in that, Kathy thinks vaguely. But you could go in any direction, it wasn't just war or women at the fringes or how consequences mount up with the minutes, invisible invisible and then overwhelming. It was permission: who gives it, who needs it. An example, should you censor pictures? What if they were bad pictures made by bad people who didn't understand. Take away their brush, put them in prison, chastise anyone who wants to look at their art. Kathy had been to see the painting that everyone was upset about. Back in May she'd gone with PJ to the Whitney Biennial, which smelt by that time strongly of rotting bologna. She didn't like or dislike the Emmett Till painting, she had strong feelings about what had been done to Emmett Till but as to what a person could or couldn't paint, no. Her books had been banned in Germany and South Africa, she was no stranger to saying things so disgusting and repellent that everyone gagged, she was like a really bitter drag queen only – surprise!!! – she had a pussy under her dress.

The markets were tanking. Everyone was jittery even especially financial traders. North Korea was threatening to bomb Guam. Kathy knew about Guam because her friend Gordon grew up there. Gordon the only man she knew to genuinely look good in a beret, hot, tight, like the kind of Beatnik revolutionary who wrote poems but could also fight. Trump's face with its white sweating eye-holes. How had all this happened? Some sort of gross appetite for action, like the Red Wedding episode only actual and huge. It didn't feel actual, that was the problem. It felt like it happened inside her computer. She didn't watch the news or listen to the radio, in fact she'd imprisoned the TV inside a cupboard she'd had specially built. If she walked away from her laptop what was there: a garden, birches, that Malcolm XXX man chatting in the queue. Walk back, Armageddon. A bird had landed in the tallest birch. She couldn't make it out with her glasses on, or with them off. 40, not a bad run in the history of human existence but she'd really rather it all kept going, water in the taps, whales in the oceans, fruit and duvets, the whole sumptuous parade, she was into it thanks, she'd like that show to run and run.

Two days passed. Asleep, Kathy came hard and woke into a grey disappointing morning. She lived here now, in her husband's house; this was her one extant bed, her own actual bed being packed in pieces in a storage unit somewhere in Cambridgeshire. Yesterday she had opened the door to three young Romanian men, boys really, who had cleaned her windows impeccably and made a mess of her worktops and kitchen floor. She slipped the oldest a five-pound note, one of the non-vegan slippery ones, because he seemed to be finding the responsibility of teaching the use of mop squeegee and cloth overwhelming. They kept ringing to say they were almost done and she'd come back to find them sitting in the garden washing pieces of the oven, 20 minutes, 20 minutes. In the end it took 4½ hours and she scrubbed the floor herself. Then she gave the keys back, then she went about bowed under recollections of the things that had happened in the house, sex mostly, some parties, a lot of miserable nights non-sleeping, a passionate interest in repainting radiators. Sébastien always came in the back gate, wheeling his bicycle, er hello, um shall we have coffee. I like you she'd once said after or maybe even during intercourse and he'd looked round the room wildly and cried I like your bed! I like your room! Matthew at New Year, shouting at Jonathan for months on end during his morning visits. For years she'd thought she was cursed with evasive non-committal distant men, my soi-disant boyfriend she'd called Stuart but now she saw she'd picked them all, that they were the bulwark between her and any actual emotional demands, at which she was not good, not skilled, she'd be one of those women who ignored their family and lavished all attention on the dog. She felt blank. She felt blank and mildly hysterical, she was itching to do something but it wasn't clear what. She wanted to get in the car and drive to somewhere entertaining and ideally hot, she wasn't prepared to bed down just yet. She wrote six emails, three dutiful, one ill-advised and then felt a little sick. Human relations, how. It was never easy to know how close to situate yourself, how open to be. The chestnut trees all had a fungus that was turning them brown. There was one directly in her eyeline, it made her feel like summer was already over, like the rot had set in. There were regions of cellulite on her upper thigh, she'd seen stretch marks on what had for 40 years been her unchangingly skinny arse, time was doing her over, she felt breathless with it. There was a literal train line at the bottom of the garden, how much more emphatic could it be? She was at the middle of her life, going south, going nowhere, stuck between stations like a broken-down engine.

Kathy was actually happy. This was the best month of the best year of Kathy's life, she was just unphlegmatic, a drama queen, sunk to the knees in her own moods. Go to Homebase, buy some paint. Paint your shed. This is home ownership, this is as permanent as it gets. The mistake she'd made as so often was to read the news immediately after waking. A Nazi march in Charlottesville complete with flaming torches and armed militias, an email from the *Guardian* headline UK family found guilty of enslaving homeless and disabled people subhead Lincolnshire gang forced at least 18 victims to work for little or no pay and live in squalor for up to 26 years. She felt sick. Stories like that displaced her, they displaced everything, how could you be happy when you knew the tendencies humans had, their aptitude for cruelty. Libyan coastguards firing on sinking refugee boats with machine guns, climbing aboard to pick the pockets of the drowning, Kathy was sick of it all, she sat down at her desk and typed Hiroshima, the flesh on the back of his hands was loose like pieces of wet newspaper she typed most of the dead bodies lay on their stomachs and were naked scorched black she typed round black balls lay in the sand she typed a child tried to get milk out of her dead mother's breasts. Maybe this last one was Kathy, the eternal orphan, the needy little girl, but it was also the world, an unshruggable burden, nastiness in small private places and out in the open, flagrant and stately. Since there'd be no end to it she might as well consign it to paper, the only thing I want is all-out war she wrote with a flourish.

★

It was midday, Saturday 12 August 2017, she ran herself a bath and fumbled a book from the small tower she'd assembled last week. She chose an extended essay by a New England novelist, a pornographer with good syntax, a lusty grammarian. It was about another novelist she liked less, it was an ardent assessment of his sentences and soul. She breezed through words like tennis, suntan lotion and adultery. Nabokov and Henry James were called into service. Then the New England novelist made an astounding statement. He said that the only good novels were written by gay men and women, that they have the gig locked, that they're streets – whole boulevards! – ahead. The gaiety was how he referred to the homosexual community, which suggested he didn't know many of them. However, Kathy agreed. What's the novel about if not getting fucked.

That afternoon, she and her husband decided to go for a walk. They drove into the countryside, not a place where Kathy spent much time. They followed a path in silence, eating blackberries as they went. A moth, her husband said. Or perhaps a butterfly. They saw a car parked at the edge of a field. How did it get there? There was a striped sheet or towel blocking the windows. Kathy, who thought about suicide a lot, wondered whether someone had killed themselves, but the car was empty. They walked a little further. There was gunshot. Bird-scarers Kathy said confidently, and saw a small fluttering thing in the field spasm and fall still. There was a fort of hay bales and inside there was a man with a gun. This was why Kathy hated the countryside. Above clouds like helium balloons, like zeppelins. Further on another man bulky in black was leading a small child with long blonde hair across a cornfield. Everything looked not-innocent, she shouldn't have come.

It was no better at home, it was worse. She watched a stream of images coming out of Charlottesville, armed militias, crackers in camo armed with assault rifles. They were chanting Fuck You Faggots, they were waving Nazi flags, they were holding up Tiki torches they'd bought in Kmart to scare off mosquitoes, disgusting putrid horror-faces, Halloween mask America. Why do men always want to punch you in the face, what was that about? The women stood on the sidelines in tight red vests that said FREEDOM right across their boobs. Nazi flags but T-shirts, sloppy, Kathy thought. Aviators and button-downs, belted chinos, pimpled white chests.

She'd been writing about Nazis since 1988, she knew what she was seeing. Let's communicate w/out hate in our hearts, Melania or let's face it her aide tweeted some hours in. The headline of the *Daily Progress*: Fire and Fury. A car drove into a crowd of counter-protestors, HORRIFYING FOOTAGE everyone retweeted, one woman dead, nineteen injured.

Kathy was becoming obsessed with Holocaust-deniers, especially the young ones, the Nazis who'd rebranded themselves as the alt-right. She kept going on the Daily Stormer or following threads. The main argument seemed to be that there weren't enough gas chambers, enough mass graves. They used words like cuck and octoroon, fag obviously, they liked testosterone and whiteness, they were anxious about having their car windows smashed. They made jokes about gassing Jews, they were like stupid boys at school except killing people and in the government, it wasn't a great moment in history, she still couldn't quite grasp how it had all come about. The Holocaust was said to have happened in the 40s, she read on a Nazi website, when information was exactly six million times harder to come by than today. Also, all of the 'evidence' was sealed behind the iron curtain, so no one could even investigate the sites where it was supposed to have happened until the 90s. On it went, talking about the absence of gas chambers, the reconstruction of gas chambers, how there were no mass graves or evidence – a sarcastic emphasis on evidence – that any more than a few people had died of starvation and disease in these work camps, how the whole thing was a *narrative* that got *fixed*. Sunday morning, 13 August 2017. There were people in the White House who believed this shit. Truly Kathy was living in interesting times.

★

Marriage in 5 days, marriage in 4 days. Kathy peeled herself from her husband and boarded a train to London. She was feeling panicky, she couldn't quite remember how to be alone, ironic since she was the poster girl for female solitude, itself ironic since she barely regarded herself as female. A fag with tits, statistically improbable but not unheard of, especially in the conglomerate-building internet era of gender dismantlement. The best thing about breast cancer was the double mastectomy, lop them both off she'd said, I always hated them. Hair cropped, skinny, flat-chested, she was a lovely dickless boy, a wrinkling Dorian Gray, fondling her jewels. Who was the drag queen who'd kept a mummified corpse in her studio for years?

Dorian Corey? No one Kathy actually liked had a stable gender identity, not really. Transitioning, she loved the word, with its sense of constant emergence and zero arrival. She was indeterminate and oversexed, a hot chrysalis, if she'd had a dick you better believe it would be perfect, at least as good as David Bowie's.

At King's Cross she took the Piccadilly to Holloway Road and walked north. She stopped at the Costa to buy mineral water and proceeded to an alley off Seven Sisters Road. The artist occupied a windowless studio. Her work was very pure and strange, she'd invented a new technique that allowed her to incorporate motion, assembling her sculptures precariously so that they toppled or burst or otherwise deviated from authorial design inside the kiln. The new pieces were kinetic and disturbing, they contained dangling entrails and slabs of bacon, hide, balls, a donkey's head, women's dainty ankles and bare Barbie doll feet, petals, guts, cloaks and various internal organs. They weren't representational, Kathy just kept being reminded of things she'd seen, rendered deliciously in the coolness of porcelain. There wasn't any precedent, maybe a garden that was simultaneously a mass grave would give you the right feeling, or some sort of body soup, out of which a white world would shortly be created. They were that frightening, that generative and grossly pretty. The new ones had a component she hadn't seen before, which looked like the spine of a dead dolphin. Kathy was not being whimsical, she'd seen the spine of a dead dolphin and this frighteningly ratcheted torted shape reminded her of it.

Studio visit accomplished, PG Tips drunk, Kathy went back to King's Cross and met Jenny in the pub. They talked about marriage, how to do it so it didn't bury you beneath all its baggage. They thought they had a handle on it, they thought they could see a way to maintaining their dignity independence autonomy style, but it was touch and go they both admitted. Place cards, stag dos, the whole thing was fucking repulsive. Someone somewhere had told her that day about hearing women say they were voting for Trump because they didn't want to work, I mean, Kathy said three beers in, could we just fucking abolish not even gender but people. I think I'm done.

Home again, she went on Instagram, Rich naked and pallid in the ruined fallout shelters of Orford Ness, somebody's courgettes arranged and lit like a Renaissance painting. Over the course of the morning she'd become an expert on neo-Nazis, she knew about the Oath Keepers and the 3%ers, she knew that cops were even crazier and more racist and evil than she'd thought, which speaking as a cop-watcher Rodney King and Michael Stewart through to Philandro Castile and Eric Garner was maximally racist and unjust. It was late, she was up in her study listening to trains and a neighbour or burglar hauling sacks of compost in their garden. Red lights, white lights, how close to the state do you want to get, do you care for the state, does the state mean anything to you at all? Kathy was a libtard, a regular schmuck, but she was also a biker bitch, a libertarian, live and let die, she didn't give a fuck, people could rip each other's faces off if that's what they wanted, only she really hated a racist cop with a gun, strip 'em and drive 'em through the streets like wild pigs, wouldn't that be the best thing to do? Outside, a man was shouting No Power No Power in a resigned voice. A new camaraderie, a green square like a meadow we can all be friends in. Kathy was tipsy and punchy, Kathy's hope is the hardest thing to hide.

*

It is now 3 days till she gets married. Her husband emails her a list of his shopping and cooking intentions plus a Word doc of the household expenses, many of which she finds immediate fault with. £200 a month for electricity, insane. Virgin TV, she won't pay that, she's been a TV refusenik since she was seven, standards have to be maintained. Cleaners, fine okay she has entered a new era. The cooking and shopping list is more endearing, it is 100% her husband's style. On the morning of their wedding, at 9:30 precisely he proposes to go to the market for salad materials, rosemary, potatoes, courgettes, and strawberries (the Oxford comma is his), and to check if the fish man is there on Saturday. Order sea bass if so, he writes (If not, buy now). At 11 he will make dressing for salad, at 11:10 he will ice their wedding cake. She has asked him repeatedly to buy a cake but he believes absolutely that this is a task only he can accomplish. They are getting married at 3pm, though this is not on his list. On Saturday, their first day of actual real married life, he will be collecting a leg of lamb and making tiramisu. Fine. Kathy will be ambling and complaining, failing to put her bowl in the dishwasher, stalking the internet, rehanging pictures. Everyone needs a job, and she understands hers. 11:10 ice cake, what a very nice man. He's taken to sunbathing naked in the garden, in a hidden zone she built for him by lugging various items of not-quite-rotten garden furniture behind the shed. He likes to lounge there with his tea and biscuits, lordly on a striped blue towel, preserving, he explains, his small speckled bottom from splinters and ants.

That evening, 15 August 2017, Kathy and her husband went out to dinner in a very dirty convertible. The driver was an old friend of her husband's, he kept asking where her pad was, he was a '60s person, loping and long-eared, the light was hitting the filth on the windscreen and he could barely see, he said, explaining why he wasn't laughing at Kathy's jokes. The light was low like a wave, a breaking gold wave, and everywhere there were plumes of dust from the combines at work in the evening fields. The man was telling her about the purple bird shit he'd found on the car roof. Blackberries Kathy said, no he said, cherries. The dinner was in a house in a village she'd driven through several times with Sébastien, on the way to a pub he'd developed an obsession with. The man whose house it was was a highly regarded even quite famous home cook, he had a wood-oven and a steely professional-looking kitchen. There was goat's curd and tomatoes, there was a tilting bowl full of razor clams and regular clams with little dots and dashes of chorizo. The clams had been purchased in Selfridge's, after a trip to the Russian embassy. The wines kept changing, Kathy was already drunk, there was loud jazz, you had to keep hold of your fork.

Guineafowl, bread sauce, Kathy argued with the long-eared man about Trump. He hasn't done anything yet, the man kept saying, which was like arguing with an ostrich about the sky. They talked about digging out basements to build libraries, they talked about literary magazines, they drank further glasses of burgundy and then abruptly there were differently tilting bowls of roast peaches and clotted cream, Kathy was jovial, she might even have slapped the home cook on the arm. She and her husband were so thoroughly drunk when they got home, so completely saturated in alcohol, that they fell asleep on their bed fully dressed and with all the lights on. She woke at 2 and rolled out of her clothes. At 6:30am she got up, mounted the stairs to her study and filled in several complicated immigration forms for the non-resident alien co-ordinator at the university where she was teaching next term. She was going back to America, soon, not for good. Movement caught her eye. There was a glossy orange fox in the garden, digging for worms. It ran smartly towards the house and reappeared with a blackbird in its mouth. A brief tussle and the blackbird escaped into a bush. The fox looked baffled and spent a moment bouncing at the bush on its hind legs. Her husband had appeared by this time, wearing a rumpled white T-shirt, no pants.

He was very warm, she pulled him back to bed. Two days to go. 53 hours.

That was the morning that white people finally realised the President of the United States was a white supremacist, he'd as good as said so, there was a cartoon in the *Guardian* of the White House with a Klan hood over the roof. Why were people surprised, weren't they listening to anything? Kathy read some threads from people on the far left, hysterical over weapons caches in Charlottesville. Here's something you need to know: Caches of weapons were found throughout Rwanda after the genocide. This wasn't about the CSA statue, but a test run for a militia takeover of a small city. I am sorry to bring you this tonight. There's a bigger plan at work here. Please don't doubt that. Take nothing for granted.

People weren't sane anymore, which didn't mean they were wrong. Some sort of cord between action and consequence had been severed. Things still happened, but not in any sensible order, it was hard to talk about truth because some bits were hidden, the result or maybe the cause, and anyway the space between them was full of misleading data, nonsense and lies. It was very dizzying, you wasted a lot of time figuring it out. Had decisions really once led plainly to things happening, in a way you could report on? She remembered it but distantly. A lot had changed this year. The people who opposed it were often annoying but that didn't make them wrong. Think how many annoyingly right people the Nazis had killed, people who said inconvenient or paranoid things that turned out to be true. They were dead and so were the cynical ironic people and the people who had refused to engage, the people who fought street battles and the people who closed their doors and came inside and preserved culture instead. Kathy wasn't sure what she would do if it came down to it. Back in the day she'd done her time in the black bloc, she'd jostled to the front, shoulder to shoulder with the bandana boys, the brick-throwers, but then she'd decided she hated them, that the whole thing was dogmatic and foolish, a game on both sides. Hard to tell now. Depends where you're standing. Like inside a synagogue, like in a headscarf at the airport. What the fuck had happened. She can see two books out of the corner of her eye. *Mother Country* and *Cruel Optimism*. Maybe she should read them.

★

Days are a ladder. The wedding cake is in two halves on the kitchen worktop. She is training herself to do cat eyes, she has purchased liquid eyeliner but her hands are shaky. Perhaps cat eyes are the province of the young and smooth-skinned. In the magnifying mirror her eyes vanish beneath deep gouges. Her body is not quite the body she would wish for. It's been all downhill since puberty, her real body is the body of an androgynous eleven-year-old, lanky and lean, built for speed. She tries on her wedding dress. There is something about it that reminds her of a dinosaur, probably a stegosaurus, a sort of inutile frill, not that any frill was exactly utile, but this one was exceptionally pointless, like a dinosaur's spine. Well, there it was: she'd marry in a dinosaur suit with uneven eyes. The house smells of coffee and new paint. The sick chestnut tree is a small conflagration on the skyline. A train horn blows. 29 hours.

She dreamt of Sébastien, she dreamt he was on a beach with Tracey Emin and then she dreamt that she was showing him an angry letter she had written to someone else, another unwilling boyfriend, and it was only afterwards that it dawned on her he would think that she was in the habit of producing these things, that she had a talent for them. Which was true, she did. Yesterday, in the car back from Waitrose she had screamed at her husband, literally just screamed, a noise without words, she was frustrated and distressed beyond language, what had it even been about? I hate you, you're stupid, she'd said over and over again, neither of which was remotely true. He was the cleverest nicest most lovable man she'd met but she was like a feral animal, she had no idea what to do with love, she experienced it as invasion, as the prelude to loss and pain, she really didn't have a clue. All day she worried that he might have a heart attack, like Hemingway's wife Pauline, who died after an argument by phone, years after they'd divorced. Why couldn't she be calm like water. I want to kill you, she'd said that, her throat had hurt all afternoon. He hated shouting, he hated all sudden noises, a dropped fork would make him flinch, if he broke a glass he felt bad all day. He wasn't fragile exactly, he was just transparent, transparently hurt or scared, closing up around himself like a starfish, a sea anemone. It was her responsibility, she was about to vow to protect him, literally sign her name to it & vice versa. Please Kathy, do this right. She'd also dreamt about a stately home, a pile of silk and linen in a garden, dusty pink and beige. There were four magpies in the birch, the same four magpies that had been fighting all week. There was a 30% chance of rain, the garden was immaculate. Four magpies and a crow, palpably irritated.

Was everything okay, was everything okay. On Twitter she wrote My inescapable paranoia, your love for yoghurt, paraphrasing Frank O'Hara. She meant it as a confession. You think you know yourself inside out when you live alone, but you don't, you believe you are a calm untroubled or at worst melancholic person, you do not realise how irritable you are, how any little thing, the wrong kind of touch or tone, a lack of speed in answering a question, a particular cast of expression will send you into apoplexy because you are unchill, because you have not learnt how to soften your borders, how to make room. You're selfish and rigid and absorbed, you're like an infant. Kathy's hair is standing up in a cowlick, Kathy is basically naked, Kathy is getting married in 7½ hours.

SWIMMING IN THE AIR

It was like a year had gone by in a single day. 18 August 2017. First Mary's dog had been attacked and had to go to hospital, then there was an accident on the A14. Everyone was late, it was intolerable, she was so nervous, her body was an inhospitable territory she could never get out of. She breathed in various places. That was what you do, you breathe. The dog's skin had been torn off on his flank, right where his leg joined his body, it was a bad wound, he'd be fine but right now he was scared and sore and about to be given general anaesthetic. Kathy loved that dog, he was pretty much her favourite person. She'd wanted him as a witness to her wedding, even if confined to a car boot and not actually able to view proceedings. Anyway she painted her eyelids with black lines that flicked at the rim. Anyway there was thunder, lightning, a biblical downpour, anyway she put hazel leaves around a china platter that had once belonged to Doris Lessing. They iced the cakes together, bickering. They stuck strawberries on, Kathy was competitive even on her wedding day.

She wore an orange coat and sunglasses, it wasn't raining, fuck it. Lime sandals. Her husband wore seersucker, also sunglasses, they looked sharp, scissored keenly against the sky. They were stressed and then all of a sudden, in the car park, they were ecstatic. NO EXIT it said in big white letters, but they didn't care, they loved it, permanence was what they were here for, they didn't want to get out. She'd forgotten her bouquet, Al said she'd get one and she did, she vanished for ten minutes and came back with ten sweetheart roses creamy pink, tied with straw, God knows how. In the meantime they'd had passport photos taken, just to get fully into the bureaucratic vibe, they looked squashed and plump and a bit glazed. There was a bell with a sign sellotaped above it saying BELL, they were all getting a bit hysterical, it was never a good idea putting her and Sarah in a room together, they'd cackle for years. Then they were off, marching to Maria Callas, I do and hereby and turn and face and forsaking all others till death. It was actually an openish marriage but yes she meant it. No one on earth could possibly be so nice.

They spent a long time pretending to sign a register with a pen that didn't have ink, she wasn't clear why. Then they did sign, then they were done. Her husband danced out the door, a cross between a cancan and a gavotte. They drank Le Mesnil, they got deeply involved in the cake, it started raining again, the doorbell rang and rang, they accumulated pink flowers and white flowers, the floor filled up with damp plants and umbrellas, they ate melon and chicken, Al had her own cake. The dog survived his surgery, that was okay. Sarah's cats had been in the wars too, especially Helix who in the end after weeks had been found to have a long stem of grass stuck up his nose. In the breaks between storms she and Leo stood in the garden and discussed the paedophile, who was maybe going to be kept on, not even kept on given a plum of a job. Leo was angry, she was angry. Back inside, they were eating more cake when someone shouted Steve Bannon's resigned. They all checked their phones. Bruce Forsyth had also died, he was older than Anne Frank, but the main news was Bannon. It had literally just happened, no one quite knew why, great wedding present she muttered to no one in particular. Confederate statues were being pulled down all over America, often in the night, mayors were just sending out orders and ripping them down. Perhaps we need a monument that lists the names of every enslaved person we can identify, in the tradition of the Vietnam War memorial the other Sarah said the next day on Twitter. Everything was hotting up, going faster and faster. At 8:30 she fell asleep on the sofa, she was going to love and honour, everywhere, indiscriminately, those would be her watchwords from now on.

They began married life by lying in bed with tea as per. Kathy was zoning out, her husband was fiddling with his phone. He was chatting away, sort of to her, sort of just keeping himself verbal company. Startup-grind is following me, I wonder why. He agitated gently over the censorship of a journal of Chinese scholarship, it's quite wrong he said and read out most of an article about it in the *Guardian*. He seemed to know all the participants. Then he found an auction catalogue and got stuck in. Little box things, little silver things, who cares. EPNS coffee pot, no thanks. Come in number 6 your time is up, Ooh I think that's an early Julia Ball, yes it is, look an early Julia Ball! Really there was nothing they liked, it wasn't their thing, miserable nineteenth-century landscapes and lithographs of cockerels. He drove out to get her breakfast, she got them both jam, plum and apricot, it was a Saturday morning, they were more actual, more legitimate, they'd bartered some-thing, swapped one territory for another, which already seemed brighter and better, more roomy. He was at home, he knew it well, but she was all fresh, she'd been uneasy for weeks, like a person on a liner, but now she was finally here she loved it, she honestly did.

They didn't have a honeymoon, they screwed it up, partly because of the injured dog they ended up in various houses in Suffolk or travelling in between with their bags in the boot, a growing confusion of CDs, maps and auction catalogues in the footwell. There was a carnival, tea, short walks, roast meat. They went to a locally famous rural auction, walked through room after room of desperate furniture, lawnmowers, mildewed prints, china vases and sagging chairs, sneezing as they went. She wanted to buy a ceramic tiger, he refused. Things in circulation, garage and attic goods, drifting miserably between lives. They drove away before the bids began.

That night, 21 August 2017, they stayed in a friend's cottage. There was crab for dinner but no tools to eat it with. Lara vanished and returned with an orange Ikea DIY set and a claw hammer. They took it in turns to smash their crabs. Kathy Googled how to eat a crab, and reported back on the zones to avoid. They were drunk. Dead man's fingers. Apparently crabs aren't poisonous anymore or obviously never were, but anyway, she was wary. She put the claws on the table and hit them hard. It was brilliant, she would have been happy to smash many more things. She hit the back of the crab as hard as she could. Nothing happened. She hit it again. A network of cracks appeared. She pried at it with her fingers, tearing out small white chunks of flesh.

All night the combines worked in the fields. When she woke at dawn, the greyish wheat was gone and the stubble was gold, the straw organised in shining lines. Walking that afternoon had felt like swimming, the air blood-warm, the apples falling on untended ground. When the combine passed the chaff poured out unstintingly, the thick dust drifting through the air like woodsmoke. The hinge of the year, picking black-berries, not knowing where to go from here. They talked about Crete, maybe a plane to Chania, maybe a bus, maybe a taxi. They wanted to prolong it, they didn't want September, they had seen a tiny hole in the sky, not the eclipse, a different one, but they hadn't been fast enough and now depressingly it was back to business as usual. Which was what, just turning words, just talk-ing, just eating cereal, the same each day. She was bored, she wanted novelty and heat, she wanted to unhook herself.

There was a photograph doing the rounds of Trump staring directly at the sun, moments before or maybe after the eclipse. She didn't like anything about him whatsoever, but she did understand why you might just want to look at the sun eye to eye. If anyone called her Mrs she'd hit them. Nothing had changed. Nothing had changed. She dreamt she'd dropped something, she dreamt she'd got keys to the wrong flat, she kept apologising. It was too fast and too slow at the same time, the low sun throwing small sharp shadows behind each clod of turned soil. Marriage hadn't solved anything, if by anything you mean Kathy herself, basic dukkha, the unfulfilling nature of existence, it hadn't stopped time, it was still all going on around her. I like to look at your breasts her husband said and she didn't speak to him again all the way home.

Back in her study, she wasted several hours looking at the comparative virtues of flying vs getting the train from DC to New York, then dowsing for an Airbnb rental in the East Village. The one she picked was one street away from her own old apartment, where she had lived in shabby splendour for many years. The bath had been in the kitchen, there was always a mild possibility of a gas leak, the internet never worked, the neighbours were obnoxious, she slept on a platform bed, spent hours of her life just corpsed there, gazing at the ceiling & scribbling down elements of her dreams. Three quarters of these bums're black or Puerto Rican. The concrete stinks of piss much more than the surrounding streets smell. She said in an essay that was St Petersburg, but she'd never even been to St Petersburg, it was New York, it was the 14x6 streets recently rebranded as Alphabet City.

Now, sitting on her sofa, she wrote: how did America begin. To defeat America she had to learn who America is. She wrote: Trump, a minor factor in nature, no longer existed. She wrote: what are the myths of the beginning of America. She was beginning to excite herself. She wrote: the desire for religious intolerance made America or Freedom. Someone was pounding on the door. The hammer, smashing the crab's back. She wanted to be cracked open, that was the thing, only on her own terms and within preordained limits. There were rules, she changed them. I love you rat paws, she said to her husband, and placed a pillow between them.

The next day, on a whim, she cut her own hair in the bathroom mirror, really just snipping at random. A boy's crop, somewhere between Charles and Diana, who in the one of the photos reproduced everywhere that week looked like a schoolboy, distinctly faggy, the prettiest in the year, with a Roman nose and wide hooded eyes, not far off Cary Elwes in *Another Country*. Kathy liked Diana, she liked hysterics and also stoics, she liked thinking of her prowling around Kensington Palace, carrying her phone in one hand, stepping carefully over the cord, maybe a glass of Chardonnay in the other. Talking to Freddie Mercury, darling I'm so bored you can't imagine, come over, okay shall I come round. Making a play of it, not Marie Antoinette at all, not even that spoiled, just needy and painful and uncontained. When she decided to leak her story she couldn't believe it wasn't possible for the book to be printed the next day, that's pretty funny but also understandable, thought Kathy, who had also railed over publishing lead times. Hungry people, puking up meringue in the palace loo, what's not to like. It was levelling, which is maybe why everyone went so mad when she died. Personally Kathy had been bombed on heroin that day, after buying an unwise bag of cut speed, but she recalled the sense of fever, the sweaty heat of it, everyone ruffled and unwise, caught up, a little sickly. Not that long ago Kathy had walked around the Diana Memorial with a poet she knew, not on purpose, they just happened to be there, and they had both been struck by how slippery and lethal it seemed vis-à-vis the many small children racing slickly through the channels. Later or maybe earlier they went swimming in the Serpentine, a first on both sides. The water was black and composed mostly of duck shit. The poet said I'm going to be a real boy now and broke away from her in a showy crawl. She watched the buildings, grey on the horizon, sad old London, diminished in the particulate plane-pollen air. There were no showers. She didn't mind, she washed in a basin but the poet, who had a date later, did. It was possible Kathy had cut one side of her hair shorter than the other. She wasn't really bothered about that either, she wondered sometimes when her polished self would emerge, elegant and capable, immaculately groomed, she was pretty composed, she'd travelled a lot, you get a sheen after a while, but still, groomed she was not.

A thing people said a lot that year, and especially the year before, x is a trashfire, also I want to burn everything, sometimes eroded to: burn everything. People were complaining about Pepe the alt-right frog but it seemed to Kathy that there had been some internet-induced desire for destruction on both sides, it wasn't the most constructive place to spend time. She was still deep in her phase of right-wing research. She'd spent the morning, 23 August 2017, reading an essay about Dylann Roof, the white supremacist with the bowl haircut who had massacred nine African-Americans in their church. He looked dumb and vacant, like hate had simply occupied a ready-made space, not that there was anything simple about it. The writer of the essay went to a plantation Roof had visited before the murders. I stood next to the dummies that are supposed to represent black people in their deepest ignominy, she wrote, and noticed that there were no dummies that were supposed to represent the masters or the mistresses of the plantation. Accompanying the article was a photo of Roof burning Old Glory in a *GOLD'S GYM* muscle top and stonewashed jeans. What republic did any of them want? One where no person was ever not the same, and therefore no one would ever get left out of account. Bitch please, are you truly that stupid? A republic worth burning 11 million illegal immigrants for, as Kathy had heard a KKK leader vow to do on TV that morning. They wanted milk and honey, the whole Biblical nine yards, and also the rivers of blood and burning cities, Slave Street up and running again, reanimating those abject bodies. It was like living in a Philip Guston painting, it was that dumb and rotten, that cartoonish, blood stains on white robes, good old boys with night sticks going on patrol, then a pile of shoes and jackets, you know exactly where the owners are.

Who is anyone right now? A friend had offered to paint them a portrait as a wedding present, they said yes of course. They went for the first sitting, two chairs, the big question was how close to set them. She was all for sprawling but the artist advised a small gap. He took lots of photos, some close some less so. This is a big commitment, he said, it's going to take a lot of time. Are you sure you're into it. They were. Kathy had modelled often, really a lot, sometimes clothed more often naked. Her husband was less familiar though honestly much better at sitting still. The room was white, glassed at the end, shelved with jars of pigment bought in Rome for 2,000 lire, a quid each, back in the '90s. Kathy loved them, she liked the dusty floor, she liked submitting to the camera lens. It was exactly like Warhol said, everyone wanted their fifteen minutes of pure attention, the camera's unwavering serious eye. She couldn't be bothered to make pretty faces, she just looked back, frank and unappealing. You have the same eyes, David said and clicked another frame.

Somewhere along the way Kathy had read an essay comparing the sexual excesses of the Marquis de Sade's novels to an office. The pursuit of both was apathy, hierarchy, repetition, endless bureaucracy. The article compared the libertines in *100 Days of Sodom* to the management committee; the children to interns and then, audaciously, to the very 8½" x 11" multi-use acid-free paper on which the workplace discourse is pitilessly inscribed. Kathy liked that pitilessly. That night the essay induced an unpleasant dream of turds in bath water. Don't read about coprophilia before bed was one explanation, but Kathy did feel somehow soiled or sullied. She drank too much, she hadn't been to the gym in weeks, she basically lived on the couch, hunched and barely breathing. She needed clean air, vegetables, she despised comfort, there were too many pastries and radiators in her life. Christ, time accumulating in rolls around her stomach. She felt like she was hastening after agendas and appointments with a butterfly net, not able to make anything stick. She was a set of eyes that feasted on hotel and airline websites, that had been her week, the entirety of her range. Then she got tired and booked a flight too early, forgetting check-in times, forgetting jet lag, forgetting body clocks and all the expertise of moving bags and bodies around the planet that she had so painstakingly absorbed over the past two decades. She couldn't even find a sublet, she didn't want to go, she wanted her own closet, her own shower-cum-bathtub, her clear cool light, her mirrors. She hated travelling, hated frizzy hair and having the wrong sweater. She stood on the brink, shivering on a diving board, I'd rather not, I need to leave.

Within 24 hours it was all sorted, flights, hotels, sublets, the works. It was always like this, abominable, impossible and then done, barely worth a thought. Kathy emailed her friends, Matt + Carl + Larry + Alex. Mi living room es su living room, Larry said. He lived on C and 9th, she loved his couch. She and Carl expressed their ongoing sorrow and concern with regard to Sinéad O'Connor, who was going through a rough time publicly documented in YouTube videos neither of them could bear to watch. Poor beautiful Sinéad. Instead Kathy put on 'Nothing Compares 2 U' and gazed in awe at that choirboy's face. She was hung-over, she'd drunk a great deal yet again, but that phase of the summer was now behind them, they'd agreed to it over breakfast, 25 August 2017, painfully confronting the wreckage of the previous night, the chicken carcass in a pool of congealing fat, the damp remains of salad, the thirteen glasses with dregs of brandy and red wine. Thirteen her husband said. There shouldn't be thirteen, and triumphantly he plucked an unused rummer from the mix. Now, they were teetotal, from this day forth they would spurn alcohols of all kinds, especially wine, even champagne. For at least a week they would be sober, their livers would shrink, they'd stop being so bilious and grumpy and fat. Kathy had put on three pounds this summer, pure booze + lack of yoga, she wrote a frantic email to her instructor begging to return. New people, married, toned, sheeny, eternal.

They decided to put the new ordinance in place by seeing no one for a day. Their new table arrived, that was exciting, they sat on the sofa waiting for it like people in line for a movie. Then there was a considerable business of putting things on it and taking them off, shifting it by minute angles, getting it all exact and then rummaging everything with a loose hand so it wasn't too perfect. After lunch they removed themselves to the secret part of the garden and took off their clothes. Kathy had three books and a catalogue about Basquiat; her husband snoozed on a lounger while she pawed through. At 3 they had a choc ice and celebrated their one-week wedding anniversary with new vows: I vow to wash up more, I vow to be less of a dick.

It was hot, it was magnificent, there were several drunk butterflies and a dragonfly her husband characteristically praised. They'd talked themselves into tatters, now they needed to recharge on sunbeams and the basic smell of grass and dirt. Definitely almost autumn, the slant of the light, the lovely rotten ripeness. Plums, blackberries, the first few fallen leaves. The small fish that had come from nowhere were slightly bigger, all black bar one, which was surely a koi, with orange splodges and a pouting mouth. Lots of roses. Did you want for anything, really? They had fizzy water, they were warm enough in their suits of skin, two animals, even cows, that just liked to stand nearby, in the same field. Let nothing happen, just for a bit, let the minutes toll in the stunning air, let us lie on our beds like astronauts, hurtling through space & time. Kathy closed her eyes. For once, Kathy had let go of anxiety.

NOT YOU

She was trying to remember the 1980s, specifically 1987. What did people know, what were they ignorant of? This was the problem with history, it was too easy to provide the furnishings but forget the attitudes, the way you became a different person according to what knowledge was available, what experiences were fresh and what had not yet arisen in a personal or global frame. AIDS, specifically, a subject with which Kathy was as familiar as anyone who lived in the epicentre of the epicentre of the crisis pre-combination therapy i.e. the East Village New York City. She remembers STD clinics, brown plastic chairs, signs dual-translated in English and Spanish, she remembers people dying in the street junk-sick or covered in the purple of Kaposi's, friends powdering their cheeks, friends emaciated, friends juggling drug schedules, funeral protest funeral protest. What she didn't remember is what exactly people knew in 1987 as opposed to 1988. She was trying to reconstruct attitudes, to understand ambient levels of prejudice and fear. Did Warhol die that year, did Liberace? And if she hadn't been there, had been instead, say, a heterosexual English boy, what different thoughts feelings insights might she have about the world now?

It was uncomputable, it was the province of the novel, that hopeless apparatus of guesswork and sup-position, with which Kathy liked to have as little traffic as possible. She wrote fiction, sure, but she populated it with the already extant, the pre-packaged and ready-made. She was in many ways Warhol's daughter, niece at least, a grave-robber, a bandit, happy to snatch what she needed but also morally invested in the cause: that there was no need to invent, you could make anything from out of the overflowing midden of the already-done, the as Beckett put it nothing new, it was economic also stylish to help yourself to the grab bag of the actual.

She needed to be more alone than she was, it was already causing problems. She kept dreaming about being in the wrong house, being in an old apartment, with the wrong furniture, in the wrong neighbourhood, with the wrong key, the place already let, a misunder-standing, you have to share. She wanted a fortress. She wanted to swim away down a cool green avenue. She didn't seem to ever go anywhere alone. Her husband's sad eyes upset her but also infuriated her, she detested being responsible for anyone else's happiness. Like can't you just figure out what you need and get it? Why do you have to keep asking me. Kathy could share, but on her own terms. On the original question, is Kathy nice, it's looking like probably no. It's not you, she kept saying, it's me, the kind of cliché she was keen to avoid. Finally she understood all the aloof boyfriends, the endless appeal of people who were only half there. She'd liked it that way, she'd liked being by herself, kept company by her old pals hankering and craving. She'd liked living in a perpetual adolescence, never having to be responsible for anyone else. Were other people as bad as Kathy? Did they wake up out of it, in shock at their own intractability, their own bad taste?

Meanwhile the fox was in trouble. Kathy and her husband were sunbathing, not in the secret back garden but in the regular declarative portion. Someone shouted Ian twice and then muscled in. Kathy was in her knickers and a sweaty yellow T-shirt, her husband was in underpants pulled both up and down to maximise sun. The neighbour was oblivious. She wanted to tell them about the fox. The fox had become in Kathy's mind a talisman, she liked to think of it moving among them freely, an anarchist who broke their things but did not exactly wish them harm, who was conscious of objects and events of an order Kathy could not possibly perceive. She liked to remember it emerging from the apple tree, wild, unharnessed. The neighbour said the fox is the culprit. It had been stealing straw and leaving it in other people's gardens, it was not a respecter of private property, it was spendthrift, prodigal, quite possibly overdrawn. She said it was this close, she said well it's eaten Lorna and Andrea's chickens. Kathy was at maximum recline, she shaded her eyes, she had never heard of these people. Her husband said it is very beautiful. Earlier her husband saw a dragonfly on the washing line and said it has a mouth just like my grandmother's. It's a new one, a totally new colour.

Other things were going on at the same time. Houston had flooded, there were photographs of a care home in which several residents in wheelchairs, elderly black women, were up to their chests in dirty brown water. The President was on it, he was using a full arsenal of exclamation marks. Kathy read a long essay on Ivanka and Jared, she was doing her duty as a citizen, keeping abreast of corruption. No one liked them, that was the gist. Who gave a fuck, Kathy thought, no one liked Putin, likeability was irrelevant, what mattered was whether you could make people numb enough to change all the laws, change the entire system, that was

86

the game. Once you pardoned a corrupt sheriff who'd openly run concentration camps for Latinos you were probably well on the way.

Numbness mattered, it was what the Nazis did, made people feel like things were moving too fast to stop and though unpleasant and eventually terrifying and appalling, were probably impossible to do anything about. She'd been reading a book by Philip Guston. On 23 October 1968, Guston had been in conversation with Morton Feldman at the New York Studio School. He'd been thinking a lot about the Holocaust, he said, especially the concentration camp Treblinka. It worked, the mass killing, he told Feldman, because the Nazis deliberately induced numbness on both sides, in the victims and also the tormentors. And yet a small group of prisoners had managed to escape. Imagine what a process it was to unnumb yourself, he said, to see it as it actually was. That's the only reason to be an artist: to escape, to bear witness to this.

Kathy dug it, even as she felt the numbness moving up her body. The speed of the news cycle, the hyper-acceleration of the story, she was hip to those pleasures, queasy as they were. People got used to them, they depended on the reliable shots of 10 am and 3 pm and 7 pm outrage. Take right now, 27 August 2017.

HISTORIC rainfall in Houston, and all over Texas, Trump had tweeted. Floods are unprecedented, and more rain coming. Spirit of the people is incredible. Thanks! I will also be going to a wonderful state, Missouri, that I won by a lot in '16. Dem C.M. is opposed to big tax cuts. Republican will win S! The next day there was a picture of him by the floods, arm and arm with Melania in serious spike heels, her blow-dry flawless. Grifters on a jolly. The man who owned the megachurch, the pastor, Kathy supposed, was getting a lot of flak for keeping his church closed. He was praying, but since people were pitching tents on roofs they felt understandably annoyed at the doors being locked on a potentially vast public sleeping space.

Was everyone getting more democratic, now things were starting to bite? Probably not, though Kathy had some small hopes. A local mattress retailer, called something like but not exactly Mattress Matty, had opened up his stores to the wet hungry and otherwise dispossessed. He was offering free mattresses, help people get back on their feet. Meanwhile Stephen Hawking had written a letter to the *Telegraph* explaining that Jeremy Hunt was about to sell off the NHS to private corporations, even though he said he wasn't. This was beginning to seem like the end game of Brexit, especially after the

Japanese non-deal, to get the country into such a dead end, an abject hole that the only thing to do was sell the public silver. If there was any public silver left – yes, Kathy thought, schools, parks, swimming pools, possibly railway tracks, the Royal Mail, definitely the NHS. The gold had gone, also electric power and other utilities, there'd been a series of pieces in the *London Review of Books* that she'd read carefully but now could barely recall beyond a slow stirring of nausea, the sense of the ground being parcelled off beneath her. Last night a steam train had gone past on the tracks at the bottom of the garden, an unexpected visitation, its windows lit gold with old-fashioned lamps. There were people inside, in glowing chambers, and she opened the door to her study and stood in the evening air, watching them shunt by. The past was gone, if you posted a letter now it took three days to reach its destination, there were definitely unpleasant changes up ahead, less money, fewer elephants, one day for sure no water in the taps. Kathy hoped to be dead by then, but she'd prefer it if the mostly benevolent life she lived was shared equally by all people. A crane in the distance, the imperative to make it over, make it new.

★

It was raining, the noise of the rain and the trains was very pleasant, Kathy had a hot-water bottle, her study was tidy. She'd left that morning intending to go to yoga but had been sidetracked over coffee and instead had gone into town, a rare occurrence, and bought a pair of orange cashmere socks. There were people in the house all the time, the noise of paint being sanded, sofas delivered, two men carrying 2 by 4s down the alley. It was the same right down the street, everyone regenerating the houses of the Victorian poor. They built up into attics and out into gardens, Kathy's husband had three buildings out there, a shed, a study and a library. They still didn't have enough space, they tore off one Farrow and Ball colour and replaced it with another. Green was briefly exposed then covered up. No one could park for skips, the world was running out of resources, it was manic, insane.

A Trump bot had mistaken a photo of Condoleezza Rice, who went shoe-shopping while a hurricane forced Americans from their homes, for Michelle Obama. Kathy was becoming obsessed with the numbness, the way the news cycle was making her incapable of action, a beached somnolent whale. No one could put anything together, that was the problem. She had recently read an article that listed all the reasons why monarch butterflies were dying, before segueing proudly into an account of taking a plane across America so the writer could cheer herself up by seeing monarch butterflies. On the plane she complained about the air pollution of jet fuel and perfume, how it gave her allergies, but she didn't connect the casual habit of flying thousands of miles with the collapse of the butterflies. Kathy didn't blame her. The equations were too difficult, you knew intellectually, but you never really saw the consequences, since they tended to impact other poorer people in other poorer places. There is no away to throw things to didn't quite work as an axiom if you were a species that depended so stubbornly on the evidence of its eyes.

The next day, 31 August 2017, was Kathy's husband's birthday. Since it was the first time ever she had celebrated someone's birthday as their wife she got up at 6:30 and went into the damp cold garden and cut him a pink dahlia, a lolly on a stick. She made tea and set out a tray, with his card, a deep-sea diver waving, and his present, profoundly expensive cashmere socks, far better than hers, which she sort of knew were a size too small. She opened his door just as he had silenced the radio and was pulling the duvet back over his head. A small animal, warm and breathy in its burrow. She climbed in beside him and cuddled up. His tea had to be made in a very particular way, it involved several implements; hers was a bag. He was extremely excited by the tray. He was chief fusser in their lives, it was good for him to receive. The socks were too small but he held them to his cheek all the same. The diver was him, waving keenly. Hello! Hello! Help!

Fortunately she had other treats up her sleeve. She'd booked a table at the River Café. They dressed up properly, eyes, jackets, better shoes. The train went through blueness, golden fields, the swag of autumn laid out on both sides. On the outskirts of London the clouds began rolling in. They had coffee at the British Library, too strong. On the tube a young mother with a wonderful expressive face was talking to a small boy. Is it night? No, we're just underground. No, I don't think this is the Highgate Tunnel, I think that's closed. At Paddington the train rose up into the air and almost everyone got off.

After Ladbroke Grove she looked out and saw the blackened skeleton of Grenfell Tower. Somehow she had not realised how many houses and flats were nearby, how many people must have watched the children at their windows. It was the anniversary of Diana's death, it was the last day of summer, everyone was talking about what they had been doing twenty years ago, that was how you defined eras, by death and dismemberment. 2017, fire and fascism, she'd never forget it, the first season of marriage, awaking into her adult life so late, just as the world was shutting up shop.

Maybe it wasn't, a last rose here and there on the road to the Thames Path, the different eras of London Corporation housing, with residents' gardens and curved deco windows. She held his hand, she had her wallet in her bag, she was capable, they both would die. That was the essence of the birthday, the oncoming inevitability of loss, she tried to mask it, that's where alcohol was so useful, such a reliable friend. She'd actually given up drinking but she made an exception today. The food kept coming, white peach bellini, squid with chilli, a plate of raw sea bass scattered with pansies, rabbit pappardelle, blue beef, panna cotta like a severed breast, a hazelnut cake, white wine, red wine, espresso. They walked home, hand in hand, kissing by the swans. They were wrapped up in five-pound notes, in their mutual wealth and good fortune, which had arrived out of nowhere, from very unpromising conditions. You cannot be immune to downfall, loss and dirt, Kathy knew, but sometimes an afternoon is separate, its own gold sphere. She got home, felt abruptly nauseous and spent the rest of the evening crouching over the toilet bowl, vomiting everything.

Death, theirs and everyone else's, was beginning to seem more likely by the day. At some point over the course of the weekend, North Korea detonated its sixth nuclear bomb. People knew because it seemed like an earthquake had happened in Seoul, China, Japan, but actually it was an atomic bomb going off underground. How did you detonate a bomb underground? What kind of space did you need, how did it not destroy everything? These were homemade bombs, a few months ago they were supposed to be impossible for the regime to achieve but now there would apparently be no end to them. The *Guardian* had six possible scenarios, none of which sounded great, especially considering neither of the two men most likely to press the button were exactly talky, exactly diplomatic, exactly sane. Kathy was in a state of despair, not just for her own life but for all the lovely creatures, humans included, and how honestly nice life could be.

They had gone to the country. It was Sunday morning, she was reading the paper on paper, with coffee, by a fire. There was a deer park outside, maybe 100 little deer with spots on their sides, exactly like Bambi except tick-infested and real, engaging in play antler-wrestling and trotting races and kneeling down to chew and all kinds of other extremely interesting and distinctive deer behaviour. Oaks too, an impeccable landscape that in itself at once depended on and concealed all kinds of colonial atrocities, seemingly natural but totally false, anyway it was beautiful and she was in it and newly awake and disinclined to have to grapple with the potential end of all life. 2017 was turning into a bumper year, a real doozy, everything arse about tit.

In the hotel sitting room the previous night, Kathy had lain on a sofa reading *Christopher and His Kind* with a carafe of red wine. It was one of her favourite books, she loved little Christopher zipping back and forward between the present day I and the Chris of *I am a Camera* and 1920s Berlin, reprimanding his younger self and thus subtly burnishing his witty and insightful present-day being. But she kept being distracted by a conversation in the adjoining room. She suggested by mime that her husband close the door, but it wasn't closable and so instead they sat there, the unwilling audience to an invisible and disheartening play. There were two people, a man and a woman. They didn't know each other, they appeared to have been drawn into conversation over dinner. The woman was doing most of the talking. She was Scottish, he was Irish, she said, they were soulmates already. He coughed a little laugh, possibly because she had the most piercing English accent Kathy had ever heard. It was impossible not to listen, her voice went echoing through the rooms, you could probably hear it from space, certainly the deer park. She was talking about Japan, how she went to a restaurant in Hiroshima, a very unfrequented restaurant down an alley, no tourists ever went there, the whole menu was in Japanese and when they left all the staff came out of the kitchen to wave them off, it was so sweet. I thought you were her agent, the man said. Her body language seemed so dead, I thought it must be a business relationship. No, said the woman, evidently stung, no, that's mothers and daughters for you, that's how they are. I don't know if you have family (ARE YOU GAY ARE YOU GAY) I don't know if you have family, children, parents, cousins, but they don't always like you very much, they think you're a fool, and you just have to take it on the chin. Her daughter was called Nadia, her daughter was not happy, not to invade her privacy but her daughter wasn't happy at all, she had a great job in marketing, a terrific job, it was more that she wasn't happy with her life.

Kathy very much wanted to be back with Christopher and Wystan, picking up boys in Berlin, she wanted shambling Stephen Spender, with his poppy-red face and his demonic little camera, but instead she was being nailed to the wall by this woman's unhappiness, it was like a juggernaut, it might never stop. It was funny, but also it wasn't, it was so miserable and fraught. Outside the moon was like milk, the deer chewed steadily, the illusion held, but this was the thing with people, they went at each other and missed, or just as bad collided and stuck. The wreckage was awful. Kathy looked at her husband. She never wanted to say another bad word, though she did twice most days, especially when hungry or tired. Could you learn to be peaceful?

Later, in the car, they were talking about three wishes, just messing around, and she said she wished everyone in the world would be gentle, that was your forties for you, losing your edge, and he said it wasn't possible. Over the course of the weekend they'd talked about the Terror and whether violence was ever justified, he'd told her about how the Republicans used to have mass-drownings in Royalist villages in France — purity, it was lethal, you had to just let people be. She wanted to do it anyway, find little spaces inside herself and ease them open.

They stopped on the way home to buy roadside flowers, yellow and pink, they had bags of cracked Georgian china wrapped in newspaper, purchased from a dear man with a wobbling head who'd once mended china at the V&A, a job he'd been given because he rescued a cat from a bramble bush in which it had become trapped, and the owner wanted, could this really have been true, to express his gratitude and happened to be the director and thus in a position to gift a job. It had been a good weekend, was the thing, infinite white beaches, infinite blue and grey-green swims, they'd held hands, she'd relaxed, it had felt like something tender and well-worn. Then they got home and saw the deck, painted an unexpected brown, and she'd screamed and screamed. Gentle humans, a new sad dream. It didn't matter if she made the tea, it didn't matter how many vases of flowers she arranged, she hurt him, she didn't have enough self-control, she was moody, nearly insane. She'd never known exactly what she wanted, but now, 3 September 2017, it seemed clear that peace was the only thing. She put the china on the shelf. Just let it all go on. Don't die. Just let me learn that love is more than me.

★

Knowing is tenuous as a swamp. When Kathy wrote that she was very sick. Her breasts were gone, she had cancer in six lymph nodes, they were all removed. I'm in the middle of dirt, she'd written. The bodies are thrown in the water. I'm with a girlfriend in a real building. I want to do more than just see. The more flights, the more forgotten.

Death: she'd been in its room, which was somehow also a NatWest bank, and then a large empty space under the ground. In the chambers on either side, other girls, with dirt in their mouths. Dead girls, girls with very white skin, girls who had bled out from razor cuts in the soles of their feet. Kathy used to live inside a fairy tale. Not now. Now she inhabits the upper air, where moods are painful to sustain. The language will be arriving later, she misreads. Language = luggage, baggage, the sadness of rain. Ashbery has died, comma, Ashbery has died.

In the paper she reads about life in a Russian prison. It is like one of her own dreams, the women standing in the cold, forbidden to wear enough clothes, sewing nametags into their coats, dressed in a sickly green, like the nurses in *Eurydice*. They are woken before dawn, they queue endlessly in the snow, waiting for punishment, watched by cameras, they mustn't fall asleep. All women are Eurydice, she thinks. The Underworld is always available. One of the women in the piece can hardly walk. Her legs are rotting. She is or rather has been a krokodil addict. Kathy looks up krokodil, a drug invented after her own first-hand knowledge of drugs. A murky yellow liquid that mimics the effect of heroin. But addicts pay dearly for krokodil's cheap high. Wherever on the body a user injects the drug, blood vessels burst and surrounding tissue dies, sometimes falling off the bone in chunks. Sometimes people say Kathy is not a realistic writer, that she is gratuitous in her effects, but she can't help feeling they are walking with their eyes closed. She didn't make the dead girls up. Or the prisons.

★

The era of the private pool has ended. Kathy has returned to the democratic republic of verruca, the damp Daffy Duck plaster in the changing room. Since Kathy, happy, is also fat, Kathy has decided she'd better reacquaint herself with exercise. It has always been a passion, physical transformation. She has tried many sorts, starvation, body-building, she has been ripped, emaciated, carved and pumped. The protruding bone thing worked when she was younger, but what she would like to manifest now is total health. Death is passé, there is too much death in the air, she'd rather reek of well-being. At the pool, which is an echoing glass box parked at the intersection of two streets, she walks across slippery tiles, assessing lanes. Regular is fine. It's a regular day, in regularly damp September. The bombs are a little more likely but she has closed her mind to that. Down the steps, briskly. It is Kathy's experience that there is always a man in the pool and the man will always wait until you have almost reached where he stands, adjusting his goggles and staring blankly, and then he will take off, kicking hard, giving you an eyeful of chlorine and feet and then proceed down the lane in erratic crawl, not letting you pass. There are exceptions, of course. Today, each time the man gets out another man gets in. They pass each other on the steps as she ploughs determinedly up and down, cutting her furrows, a screw-kick tilting her left-wards beat after beat. She tightens her abs, she makes herself a line that flies, she watches the clock, drives herself on. It's raining, outside, but she isn't really any-where, losing herself in repetition, in muscular effort. She swims a kilometre and gets out, not panting at all, even though she nearly had an asthma attack that morning running up two flights of stairs. Maybe swim-ming isn't really exercise. It's the boys' bodies she likes, the twinks in goggles with long legs and triangular backs. She cruises idly, a disaffected shark.

On her way home, Kathy crosses several roads, waiting if there's a car, running if there's room. Halfway home, she is startled to discover that a car, instead of braking slightly to let her by, has instead accelerated. She runs but he keeps driving, steering straight at her. For a second they make eye contact. A white man, 50s, glasses. You fucking twat, she screams. Another man says something, but she is ten paces away before she realises it was take his number plate, and by then it's too late. Kathy's husband is standing in the street when she gets home but he is not interested in her story, not solicitous and alarmed as she'd expected. She was planning on playing it cool, but since he is unbothered she finds herself underlining the danger she was in, an exchange which is unsatisfactory on both sides. Bye bad love, he says to her as he leaves. She suspects he's going deaf but he denies it, he is absolutely and completely certain that it's just he can't hear her through the wall/ over the tap/the tumble dryer/the washing machine, and anyway doesn't she know she speaks quietly and very fast. What, she says and puts her hands over his ears. I can't hear you, what did you say?

She forgot her goggles so she had to hold her neck up so now it hurt. Cause and effect, quite simple. People were told Brexit would be good so they voted for Brexit and now all the EU citizens would be sent home, according to a leaked document. Apparently Jacob Rees-Mogg would be the next Prime Minister, he went on *Good Morning Britain* and explained pleasantly that he thought abortion should be illegal even for rape and that he would like to ban gay marriage. Kathy hated everything, her head hurt even after two coffees, she couldn't abide smiling men policing women's bodies, smiling men deporting immigrants, smiling men telling smiling lies on daytime television, it was all so tawdry, the endless malice of the polite right. Her back hurt, her spine hurt. At the weekend she was going to a party with people who had openly praised Enoch Powell, at the weekend she was going to a party with people who had said of refugees crossing to Greece, it's ridiculous, they should just bomb the boats. That was when she knew Trump was going to win, that was when she knew the country would vote Leave. Her head was breaking into pieces, she lay down, got up, was violently sick and subsided into a gentle, unexpected sleep.

The headaches lasted days. The left side of her body felt separate from the right, maybe she was having a stroke, maybe a tumour had activated in her brain. What she knew about illness was that it went on mostly beneath the waterline, you didn't really know the extent of damage until it was too late. The interior of her pelvis was a mess of scars, anything could be travelling through her lymph, accumulating, coalescing, bent on its own malignant work. Anyway she went to London, nauseous and wobbly. She couldn't find her sunglasses, she had to face the world bare-eyed. The orange socks were a compensation, they made her feel safe. At King's Cross she took the Metropolitan line to the Barbican, dark into light, a scattering of rain, and walked through the underpass to the cinema.

Outside she met an estate agent in a denim shirt and expensive plimsolls, with dark floppy hair. I'm not really an estate agent, he told her, I studied geography. Five people in our office went to the Courtauld. I'm a real Barbican geek. Kathy was also a real Barbican geek. She loved that building. It was the future and the past entwined. She couldn't afford the flat, not really, but she knew it was supposed to belong to her. It was on the third floor, they went up in an elevator, no piss, everything was concrete and groovy, neither sleek nor decayed, just there and amiable and impassive. The flat was perfect, a peach. One single room, with an enormous window opening onto a concrete balcony full of plants. There was a school beyond, the first or maybe

second day back children racing in circles and screaming. Kathy could live with that, also basketball courts
and towers, she was a fan of dense and segmented out-
in-public lives. There was a bed tucked discreetly in a
corner, fine, and a kitchen that can't have been touched
since the day the builders moved out. F2A, the estate
agent's particulars said, with an original Brooke Marine
kitchen, fitted for a yacht. Everything shipshape, with
the abundant pleasures of the needful and compact.
There were cupboards by the front door, you opened
one and found your post, you opened the other and
deposited your trash, which was swiftly removed. Kathy
had always wanted to live in a Heath Robinson house,
she was frantic to have it, even the taps were dotable
and dear, little stainless-steel rabbit ears.

All the rest of the day she added up numbers in her
head. They couldn't afford it, or they could afford it but
not if anything happened, like interest rates or illness or
a compelling holiday. Anyway she was wary of disrupt-
ing their happiness, capsizing contentment, scuppering
the perfectly adequate ship of their current house in
which they both generally spent every night. Would it
be strange to part so soon? Kathy always claimed she
wanted a home, but actually she had a mania a genuine
addiction for dividing her life between two places, she

couldn't help it, it was how she was built. A migrant bird, she was compelled to fly from town to town, wheelie case in tow, always lacking one or another essential implement, a charger, jacket, umbrella, scarf.

On her way home she met Charlie for tea at the BL. Just before he arrived – oh my God, I'm 127 seconds late – the estate agent's particulars got whisked up in a little breeze and were swept across the plaza. A passing man trapped them impressively between his knees. I saw the whole drama Charlie said, and kissed her in a cloud of patchouli. Charlie's patchouli was made by nuns, it was very exclusive. He and her husband and Joseph were the best-smelling men she knew, no one else came close. Furthermore Charlie had a very covetable umbrella, orange with a bamboo handle. When she finally got home some hours later she realised her husband had the same model but in black, lurking invisibly in the umbrella well in the hall. Her phone, which never ever rang, had rung perhaps a hundred times. Mercury must have been in acceleration, she thought, people she hadn't heard from in months were suddenly frantic to be in touch. So r u married now, Lili asked. You canny coo, Stuart said. She told everyone about the flat. Lili's son wanted sneakers for his birthday, he loved Vans, she promised to source rare ones at Dover Street

Market. She was experiencing one of those occasional upswells of love, when she suddenly felt satiated on a neurological and also soulful level, enough and not too much pleasant information saturating the synapses in her brain. Kathy in the autumn, Kathy midway, Kathy who has come home, who has enough to be going along with and who must now decide how to spend the small remaining days.

★

It was a party. 9 September 2017, 22:30, the fringes of the map. Things under discussion: super-Tuscans, wine nights, life in the City in the '80s and '90s, weddings. It wasn't Kathy's crowd. There was intrusive background music, she was wearing fishnet tights, Patti Smith was singing 'Because the Night', unlikely. Kathy couldn't eat but said yes to every drink, which was why at 9 the next morning she had a port hangover and could barely open her eyes. Her husband complained that he had a very dry mouth and then pulled some damp blue threads from his mouth and looked surprised. Who knew what had happened to them while they were asleep, ajar, defenceless? They were in a hotel room of such monumental ugliness it seemed an achievement in its own right. The bathroom glittered, the mirrors were made from moulded plastic, like a cheap child's toy of Versailles. There was a bar beneath them called the Log Cabin, outside which young men shouted until far into the night. At 5, a barking dog woke the entire hotel. What were they doing here? Just drifting, accepting their fate, not saying no, saying yes.

The other main topic of conversation was nuclear war. Why doesn't America just say to Kim-Ing, Kim-uh-ing, that he's a big boy now, well done, that's obviously what he wants. What I don't understand is why they don't just nuke him into oblivion. They don't know where the missiles are Kathy said in a woman's voice, which was inaudible in this and many other circumstances. I didn't recognise you, a man she had known for decades said. I'm wearing make up, Kathy replied.

What was good was the hills, the deep, densely wooded valleys, with flat shallow streams and grazing assorted cows and sheep. What was good was the clear air, brushed now and then with rain, the fast-moving green. They kept stopping at churches, they pulled in when they saw antique shops and sifted through boxes of grimy Spode and foxed hardbacks from the century before last. The past hung heavy, they breathed it in, it was good to experience the density of time. Everything was blown or shot or on the wing, the last martins skimmering above slate roofs, the oaks so dogged by their shadows they looked like chess pieces, rook to king.

Home, several motorways later, Kathy picked up a book and read a few pages at the beginning and then turned to the end. There was a run-on list of deaths, among them they found I could read and they dragged me out to the barn and gouged my eyes before they beat me. The tide of cruelty in the world was drawing in, it was impossible to ignore. The waters were rising in Miami, Tampa, Naples. You could not possibly stay at home, but the police had announced that if you had an outstanding warrant, you would be arrested at the shelter. People seemed to warm to this kind of cruelty, they thought it was tough, they liked it. Kathy foresaw a future run by strongmen, she saw the poorer nations of the world obliterated by climate change, she saw the liberal democracy in which she had grown up revealed as fragile beyond measure, a brief experiment in the bloody history of man. No surprises there, she always thought it was a veneer, dependent on cheap food, plastic, oil, flights. She was not flabbergasted but she was scared. She was finding it hard to sleep, she had perpetual headaches, she knew she shouldn't read the paper, but she snuck looks from the minute she woke up. What's Putin doing, what's happening in China, in North Korea, in the US? How's the car-crash of Brexit proceeding, how are they getting along with changing all the country's laws in secret, how much do we hate foreigners today, who's winning? Kathy was finally comfortable, Kathy was practically as secure as anyone can be, and still she was riven by despair. In the House of Commons, MPs barracked Caroline Lucas for asking apropos Irma when we were going to get to grips with climate change. They actually shouted Shame. This is how it is then, walking backwards into disaster, braying all the way.

Kathy had always mapped her dreams. She mapped the houses of the dead, she'd been doing it for years. She got out her notebook, wrote Its walls were painted with manure, I was the only human here. She wrote about rooms that were flooded with shit, she wrote about ruined houses, she wrote about children buried underground. Swamps, alleys, dead roads, dead leaves, spit and shit. Oil fires in the distance, a bank off the Tottenham Court Road that wouldn't give her money without a passport, but she couldn't find her passport. She dreamt that she died in Mexico, she dreamt that she had no health insurance. She dreamt that there were many rotting bodies under the water, she dreamt the density of the smell. She woke choking, a pain in her belly. The doctor said to her we need a stool sample, she gave her a plastic bag. Phones featured. In the dream of her death she was like a child, she called herself Janey. She would like to be bottle-fed, she is a bottom, she is a baby, she is on the edge of a void, speaking neither into nor out of it. There is nothing here but rain. She spends a whole day looking at coats. She wants to find a kind of language where she won't be so easily modulated by expectation. In the dream she passes through rooms without doors, the stairs lead into the ocean, Mark is here, she has to call but the shop has changed its number. The sense of effort, but no target. In the dream of her death she is very drugged. She spends a day in bed. It's wasted time but what time isn't.

Every morning she waits on the beach to see what the tide has brought in. The return of torture in Turkey's crackdown, the ongoing repatriation of UK law, facilitated by Dennis Skinner, a disappointment. The lynching of an eight-year-old mixed-race boy in New Hampshire. According to the victim's grandmother Lorrie Slattery, he was playing with a group of children and teens when they began to taunt him with racist epithets and throw sticks and rocks at him. One of them climbed on a picnic table and they tied a rope taken from a tyre swing around his throat and kicked him off the table. He swung back and forth three times before he was able to free himself. None of the teens came to his aid. A photograph accompanied the story, purple welts on a small neck. Meanwhile Kathy was sitting at the table, two empty bowls of muesli in front of her, a vase of dahlias, nearly dead, a bracelet, assorted magazines, bowls of fruit, light bulbs and books. Outside, the ragged autumn garden, overblown flowers, long, comfortable shadows. A passing train. Each day she sensed something creeping nearer. If it was happening to someone, it being unspeakable violence, how could she be happy: the real question of existence. The knowledge was a splinter in her own corporeality. Would this be a moment she looked back on later, damaged in an alley or locked in a cell? Something was approaching. Kathy could not settle. She knew. She knew.

Maybe it was better to sit down on a sofa, with a small new dog. The new dog that Kathy had access to was a Labrador, eight weeks old, russet-coloured, therefore Rufus. She went round to have tea with him, then again a few days later. On both occasions he spent a full minute cowering in the kitchen, avoiding eye-contact, before resuming his puppyish duties. He was chubby and had giant paws, like slippers he kept tripping over. He was too small to climb a step, he was just the right size for riding around in someone's arms, he looked smug and delicious, lounging by a Missoni blanket, a pedigree, calmly submitting to his Bruce Weber shoot.

There'd been a storm the night before, Kathy had woken in the dark to the sound of tearing. She kept pacing about, she couldn't settle, she'd switched pillows five times. The next day her jaw ached, as if she'd been biting down for hours. The house reeked of paint, it was low-grade toxic just to sit in the kitchen. Furniture kept disappearing, the garden was vanishing under foliage, damp, green, rust-spotted, unplanned. She had decided to sell her flat, a supposed investment, again. She had decided to buy a new one, again. She wanted a dog, long-legged, long-nosed, she wanted a new coat, a new figure, a new lease of life. Feet that were going somewhere, the good sleep of the weary.

Kathy was repulsed by her own indolence, she had a perpetual sore throat, Kathy never stopped agitating towards the future. She wanted someone else's life, ideally an architect called Ben Pentreath, whose rented rectory in Dorset she coveted unbearably. She spent several hours gazing at pictures of his dahlia borders, beech tree, cow parsley, churchyard, Georgian hall table, olive candles, Ravilious prints, old china, peach, hot pink and yellow and red striped tulips, and felt lust curdling in her chest. Things, she liked them more and more. Old things, haphazardly arranged, like apples fallen from a tree, that casual, that lordly. She wanted box balls and an orchard, maybe a lake, she wanted oaks and cold stone. Maybe possessions were like beauty, they made you impermeable. Kathy loathed permeability, she wanted to be gilded, I mean everyone did. The thing about wrenching her heart open was that suddenly loss was everywhere, in the window boxes of geraniums on Kingston Street, in the conkers that had blown gleaming into a skip. Fuck September, with its mournful air. Kathy wanted to bed down by a fire and not leave the house till March but she was flying back to America in ten days. Conveyancing, boarding pass, papers to grade, hotel reservations in Virginia and DC. Some little well was empty, it was weird. Kathy had definitely been this tired, maybe not this scared.

PAPERS & PAINTS

Good, a new day. She woke several times in the night, boiling hot, and threw the covers aside. The sheet was burning, light seeping in through orange then blue chinks at 2 and 4. In the true morning she surfaced a little, resting between dreams and the radio, bobbing like a lobster pot. Missiles, Korea, Japan. Later that day there was a bomb on a tube train. Photos of the bomb circulated online, a bucket full of wires in a Lidl bag, still burning. She had been writing a will when she saw it, she was future-proofing herself. Walking along the pavement it occurred to her that people who had children probably felt considerably more afraid and she was abruptly abashed at her own selfishness. She never liked people who bred making claims on the future, as if they had made a heftier investment, but actually they had. Her investment was tulip bulbs, a few books and now her husband, his dear wrinkled cheek. I know I must stay alive until Wednesday at 12, he said as he left the house. This was when the will would be signed. Yes, she said, but in ten decades' time.

Earlier that week, 14 September 2017, she had been

on a jury for a queer art show. She saw multiple Grindr portraits in pencil, pen and pastel, she saw multiple gas masks, multiple butt cheeks and assholes. Is it really so transgressive, is it not getting tired, a little bit samey. Kathy liked a drawing of a boy foreshortened and naked like Holbein's Christ, and a photo staging the death of a drag queen called Tracey Ermine, floating in the sea off Kent, her ruby slippers protruding from calm blue water. Kathy liked saying YES and NO, she liked drinking coffee and scrolling through jpegs. Later, she walked through Notting Hill in the dark, the enormous polished houses. A boy in a suit, screaming into his phone, lay down on the platform at Ladbroke Grove yelling I AM JUST SO TIRED. She was with her husband. On the train, a man asked them in broken English if he needed to change at Edgware Road. No they said, then later yes. They got off together. He had a nice worried face and a large bag, he was from Hamburg, not so far away her husband said. But all the distances had grown in the last year. The feeling of foreignness blew around the carriage. She liked the man, she smiled at him as they left. You make divisions between people, countries, races, and out of the gaps the warheads emerge. It was that simple, she was watching it happen with her own eyes.

Later that night, upstairs, she wrote in an email to her solicitor I would like to be cremated. She typed the words then went downstairs and burst into tears. I don't want to be cremated she said to her husband, nearly wailing. I don't want to be dead. They were setting all the doors to shut neatly behind them, it was expensive to think this closely about your own demise.

Meanwhile, the door was also closing on a variety of human enterprises, replaced by automated alternatives. Everyone was very angry about a thing called Bodega, which replaced the need to go out into the street and through the door of an actual bodega, there to purchase Tampax, Blue Moon, Häagen-Dazs, pretzels, Advil or whatever else you needed to survive the day, with some sort of automated internet-enabled kiosk that contained all the essentials and didn't require you to walk, speak or dig through your pockets for quarters. Then there was a hoo-ha over facial-recognition software, which was actually two stories, one about the new iPhone, whatever thought Kathy, and one about an academic study that wanted to find out if you could tell people were gay based on their faces. You only have one face, Kathy's friend Tom kept saying. You have infinite passwords, ten digits, one face. The face is not a sensible key for a phone, never mind what regimes might do with their homos.

In this atmosphere it was becoming increasingly hard to feel real. Kathy felt daily more like a helium balloon, untethered, barely attached. About to give a talk, she'd found herself breathless and numb down one side. She'd had to go into the street to do some breathing in a doorway. She wasn't nervous, she was just not real. It was like that all the time, she just noticed it more when she was with other people, the movements of her speaking face. She cut her hair again with almost blunt scissors, why. You look dreadful, her husband said, you look like Henry V, and she felt dunked in shame. The scissors thing, it was kind of self-harming, yes, but it was also just wanting to make something happen, to get control over at least one aspect of tangible reality. She could have dug the garden but she was too lazy, nursing an on again off again flu that manifested mostly as midday exhaustion and extreme temperatures between midnight and one. They were both having bad dreams, they were both headachey and queasy, they ate a lot of orange cake and then experienced mild regret.

The hair needed fixing. Fixing it required going to a place with mirrors and Kathy was incapable of looking at herself in a mirror while being looked at by another person, this was probably the root of the self-cutting issue, but also another manifestation of the unreality business. She didn't want to go back to America, that was the thing. In her mind America had become death, a crossing she did not want to make. What if the entire country or just the East Coast was annihilated in a missile strike. How would she get home. In their dreams lost luggage, trains making unsigned stops. I dreamt I was being tortured her husband said, and wouldn't say more.

18 September 2017. At 3 she went to Chantal's studio, Northern line to Angel, walked along the canal in the rain, the water very green, reflecting willow leaves and tower blocks indiscriminately. Her feet sounded good under the bridge, her strides ringing. Chantal was wearing a blue mohair cardigan covered in paint, her hair up in a scrappy twist. The studio was full of work, two enormous canvases in the corner of Chantal in her pants with her daughter, apple-green ground like Degas, her eyes very bloodshot. On the floor there were dozens of cut-out commuters, a whole population. They both liked the man at the end best, in sandals and kurta, stylish and sharp, stepping out into bright air. Apple green was everywhere, in little chinks

under people's eyes. It made everything look eerie and modern, like electricity or the internet was somehow infiltrating the air, the breathing ground, the actual backdrop to their lives. Kathy loved the cut-out people, roughly drawn, curled into ovals, their body parts contained in space. He knew, Chantal said of Vincent van Gogh. It was all right. They were talking about new work, what happens when no one likes it, what sort of conclusion you should or shouldn't draw. Chantal pulled out books, a series of tiny paintings of water towers, she described paintings of men in pants and paintings of men pissing, she brought in Guston's shoe paintings and Paula Modersohn-Becker. Together they looked at a Renoir of Julie Manet as a child, her face as it smiled opening sideways, actually very like the cat in her arms. They talked about Vermeer's use of underpainting, how he let the light leak through, they talked about a single yellow sleeve. As they talked they ate very quickly cupcakes from the Hummingbird Bakery. I was greedy as a child they both agreed. Kathy was scooping up pink icing with her finger and shoving it in her mouth. Later that day Mary-Kay said when I was a child my mother called me a snake. A sneak Andy said. No no, I was never a sneak. A snake.

After the studio Kathy walked right across town,

nearly to the Barbican then right through Clerkenwell and down St John Street to Farringdon Road. She walked up Rosebery Avenue and Gray's Inn Road and overshot and had to come back by Mecklenburgh Square. Her husband was waiting on the corner of Rugby Street in his mac and hat. A man came up to me and asked me where I bought my jacket, he said. He was very proud. She made him go into the Folk shop, she tried on a coat, a jacket and a sweater, the coat was the best, it was superior and serious, also cosy. They had time to kill, they ate chicken wings and drank wine and discussed plagiarism, whether it really mattered or not, Kathy thought no. I mean words, they're like paint, they're like Degas's apple-green ground. You take what you find, it's all material, I mean what is art if it's not plagiarising the world?

The talk was at 7, everyone was there. There was a lot of news moving around the room. Charlie and Rich were getting married, that was great. Mitzi was wearing the most beautiful coat, Colman's mustard, fastened with a lovely old leather belt. They saw Claire and Steph, also a girl with a pinched Jane Eyre face and very tightly drawn-back hair who Kathy recognised from photographs. She was listening to the talk, drinking cheap wine, but she was also thinking about the pictures in Chantal's room. Dealers don't like babies, a hulking white back like the flank of a whale.

★

The theme of the week was art, not on purpose, it had just panned out that way. The Basquiat show was at the Barbican. Rich appeared while she was queueing to buy water. Was it a good show? It was nondescript, it felt all the time like something better, more open might be going on in another room. Could this be it, these low ceilings. The paintings looked congested, sort of immaterial. What she really liked was a series of photographs by Warhol, something human going on there, public affection at the very least. Basquiat nuzzling an old dog, Basquiat swinging from a lamppost, Basquiat's face concealed beneath a Venetian mask made maybe from tinfoil, maybe from gold leaf. They spent a while trying to identify people in a set of Polaroids with a couple of strangers, both women. Debbie Harry, Klaus Nomi, Madonna, Grace Jones, for sure that's Keith Haring. Rich got Anjelica Huston, she looked very lean and imperious. Madonna was a baby in a lavender wig. I used to live in New York in 1981, the woman next to them said. She had a bob and bulky black clothes, the sort of air that made you think she might

122

be famous, though later Kathy looked her up and found very little. It wasn't dreamy enough, that was the thing. Though hypnotic to watch the camera panning along beneath the old West Side Highway, Basquiat spraying lines about cotton on a hoarding by the sugar factory. Kathy collected words, armadillo, Avenue A, war, Wall Street, she collected body parts, she liked the bits in isolation but not the faces topping torsos.

Outside the water in the pool was green and the balconies were luxuriant as usual, draped in foliage, bright with geraniums, maybe also begonias. Kathy was late, she had to go to another gallery, she was walking with very long strides, sunglasses on, trying to get one over on the clock. Her meeting was supposed to be about art but actually it was gossip, this often happened, presumably not just to her. She ate a bendy biscuit, drank what her seventh glass of fizzy water. Stories about brothers, nephews, dealers, collectors, stories about people arriving too early, people being embarrassed, being on the outside and trying to get in, only later it turned out the outside was smarter. That was Kathy's take too, also that it didn't really matter where you situated yourself since the centrifuge of history would eventually pluck you up and switch you round. It was the thing right now to take people from the outskirts, the wallflowers if you like, and try and look at events through their eyes. No one cared about Napoleon or Darwin, it was more interesting to be obscure, almost unheard of, a failure, a total creep.

On the tube Kathy kept getting glimpses of people's papers, take down hate sites in two hours or else, an earthquake in Mexico, some sort of minor or minor so far coup in Spain. She read an essay about dementia on her iPad. Was this what she was scared of, her husband receding into the blind alleys of memory loss? He was twenty-nine years older than her, she worried about blood clots, bowel cancer, a heart attack, a sudden fall. He had five aneurysms, at any minute one could rupture and kill him, just like that. One had already been operated on, she'd seen him after surgery, unconscious and intubated, his little white face absolutely drained. For weeks he'd been incapacitated, bedbound then hobbling and brave. He had sleep apnoea, that could be fatal too. It had killed Carrie Fisher. She woke him in the night to check that he was breathing, she just wanted to keep his company for as long as she could. The world was good with him in it, awful, fearful, but also secure, she raced up the road to get back to him, even if she didn't speak much or snapped she delighted in his presence, the way he was always so amenable, so keen to please, his handsome mouth, the dear little bristles around his ears. He'd painted the deck when she got home, bending at the waist on account of his artificial knee. He was very tired, he went to bed almost immediately, it was only 5, and she sat upstairs in her study alone, not unhappy, her fingers moving, watching the hazy yellow light, the golden leaves. I never know how to say goodbye, she wrote. We never do, do we? Just say 'Goodbye.'

Writing, she can be anyone. On the page the I dissolves, becomes amorphous, proliferates wildly. Kathy takes on increasingly preposterous guises, slips the knot of her own contemptible identity. I gave the old guy a dirty look. I'm not fucking you, I'm your enemy. I know my grandmother hates my father. I love mommy. I know she's on Dex. I didn't feel frightened yet. I myself never commit murder, I'm constantly drunk, I never despair. I'm as normal as any moral person. As soon as I was clean, again I started haunting clothes stores. I grew up wild, I want to stay wild. I felt very happy when my sister's huge hat, while we were both in an auto, flew away. I who would have and would be a pirate: I cannot. I who live in my mind which is my imagination as everything – wanderer adventurer fighter Commander-in-Chief of Allied Forces – I am nothing in these times. Grief saturates her words, she can't stop it, she writes about rotten meat and rape, raw sewage, she writes about mothers and fathers and little girls, she writes I'm banging my head my head into a wall.

★

It was her penultimate day in England, 21 September 2017, and her husband was up for a prize. He went to bed cross and nervy, he woke up cross and nervy. The decorator had returned. Did you know you have a parking ticket, he called from the door. Her husband was livid. He had parked on double yellows she observed reasonably, but he did not think it was reasonable at all. I LIVE ON THIS STREET, he shouted. IT'S MY STREET. Anyway there weren't any spaces from here all the way to St Philip's Road. He couldn't work out how to seal the parking-fine envelope and that made him even crosser. He didn't want to go to London or to read, he didn't want the deflation of not having won something he hadn't asked for in the first place. She felt for him, his prickles and bristles, which were so much less pronounced than her own, nearly invisible, worn smooth with age.

All her emails angered her. She walked down the garden and snapped the last dahlias, fiercely. The lawn was full of little heaps of coiled mud. Worm casts. Upstairs, she looked them up. Earthworms are herm-aphrodite animals that pair up to exchange semen. Eggs are deposited in the soil in lemon-shaped egg sacs. Worms sounded fun, a regular orgy on the greensward, she for one would not seek to prevent them.

Her husband was hunched at his chair, his head poking forward like a turtle. You're filling the house with your nervousness, Kathy told him. You're making a complex architecture of anxiety and fear. He was very twitchy, they both were. She wanted him to win and she also thought as he did that prizes were dreadful, that comparisons had no place in art. Still, they shouldered on. He left first, damp-palmed in corduroy. She couldn't find the right clothes, it was one of those days where her skin and hair felt coated in a thin layer of grease, when nothing hung right. Her socks had holes, oh well. She loved him, that was her dress, each element a sequin. She fell asleep on the train, she got off at Embankment and walked across the bridge, pausing to inspect a damp shirt caught in a railing. She met him in Eat, fed him bolognese at an Italian chain on the Southbank. The realisation of the grandeur of the occa-sion crept up on them slowly. Girls were getting into lifts in silk dresses and heels. There were long queues for press tickets. He was focusing his nervousness on some fruit plates he'd seen in the green room, which would apparently be removed at six on the dot. They had pineapple and melon, he told her sadly. She sent him on and queued alone.

The foyer filled up. Alex was at the bar, also Rebecca. Jack was somewhere in the building, she hadn't seen him since they kept frequenting the same cafe in New York. Amy, Katherine, maybe Chris. She was too jumpy to talk to anyone, she held her phone like an alibi and snuck round the back to the second-floor bar to sink a secret beer. Her ticket said C9. The tannoy was demanding haste. Then someone was on stage mourning the death of a poet, not Ashbery, and then there was her husband in his washed and worn old jacket, looking pleased and very shy. He read last, and when he got to a line about an entire bowl she gasped. Every word came out clean. We're a monstrous pair of crows, devoted to a singular being.

All the poets filed off stage. Her attention was caught by a green silk skirt, a mustard dress. But he'd won! It was his name. As he climbed back up a man behind her said he *has* got a nice face. Earlier the same man had been talking apologetically about Times Square, that there were too many people. Well there were too many people and his face was fantastic. He hadn't prepared a speech, of course. Thank you, he said. Thank you all. She couldn't get to him for ages, and when she could there were people intersecting and also in the verges. Peter said I'm Peter, I know you're Peter, she told him reassuringly. They waited a long time for a drink and drank them too fast, he was talking to a former student and was so happy he honestly couldn't get a word out. Briefly they saw the party, luckily train-wise she knew the quickest place to get a cab. It was all stops and starts, Waterloo Bridge, Euston Road, talking of all things about the paedophile. They couldn't sleep, they were too excited, they lay there whispering and making up songs, I love you, she said and placed herself entirely in his arms.

The next day was the equinox, the next day was her last day in England. Entirely unencumbered sky, the blue of flags and sailors. There was a heavy dew, she had an unfortunate headache that ran through her left eye and out the base of her skull, a metal bar with spikes. She had to collect currency and pack, she had to wrap up her life and sail away in her small boat, the one she now disparaged. She didn't want to be alone, she was done with it, it was yesterday's gig and no doubt tomorrow's. I'm going to be sick she said and ran upstairs and was. The pain was intense, she rocked under the duvet, mumbling and weeping. Then it lifted enough to dip into her emails, while he lay beside her crooning. Now this is where we live and when you come back it's our eight-week wedding anniversary, and an eight on its side means infinity so then we're permanent, which wasn't true but was nice to think about.

The headache passed, it got smaller and smaller until she forgot it. She tried to check in but there'd been an error with her ticket, someone had typed her date of birth in wrong, reducing her to 38. She rang American Airlines and was given a complicated list of things she'd need to do to be able to fly. She did them, but apparently it was the wrong list. After multiple conversations a man with a beautiful voice told her it was going to be okay. You have your ESTA? You have a valid passport? You gone be okay. Earlier that blue afternoon she had gone to the post office for her money and waited behind a woman who was trying to send mail to California. Next time you have to fill in a customs form, the postmaster told her. Customs can be very pedantic. He said something else and at the door she called back I'm not Japanese. I thought she was Japanese, the man said, baffled and clearly a little hurt. Maybe she's Korean. She looked Japanese. He counted

Kathy's money very carefully, he had a little pad to dabble his fingers but it wasn't enough, he found a bottle of water lurking behind the till and moistened the pad. Do you see what I'm doing here, he asked her. It's so I can go faster. Fifty fifty twenty twenty ten five one. The queue was long, it is not easy to get away.

That night she moved beds three times, she kept waking up thinking someone was in the kitchen. She came in to him at 1:30, his fumbling hand found her and hung on. She listened to him breathing, the long apnoeic gaps. She wasn't the first person to do this, she wasn't even the first person to write down what it felt like. She was breathless with love for him, the warm sleeping animal, the golden eyes that opened and peered at her fondly. Pip, he said. My Pip.

He woke her at 7:30 with tea, back in her own bed by then. 23 September 2017. They clung together. It was unprecedented, this departure. She'd never left a husband behind before. He was driving her to the airport, I am, that's all there is to it, even though she already had a train ticket, even though she was mad with terror lest he die in a crash. The cases were assembled, they both zipped up, all the chargers were aligned between socks and knickers, nobody could contest that she had her stuff, minus the Gucci loafers that wouldn't fit and which she'd regret for weeks to come. They were quiet in the car, clutching hands and fiddling with the aircon, the trees small yellow torches, sometimes advanced to scarlet flares. It was England, she'd miss it, even as it became unrecognisable, officially racist. The worry about checking in was overwhelming her, they hit traffic on the M40, she counted each minute and yanked at her lip. But it was all fine, Pip it's all fine, they parked and wheeled, they had plenty of time.

At the baggage drop a young yawning man took her passport. You look tired, she said. I am, but I also have something in my eye. He scrubbed at it like a child, interrogating her about her plans, the consecutive days she'd spend doing this and that. She wanted to be through and home, he stamped her ticket, she was good to go. They had time for a coffee, no one could stop them, they had a whole ocean of minutes before he had to leave. This is very watery he said, and biting into a brownie this contains orange essence. She'd never loved anyone before, not really. She'd never known how to do it, how to unfold herself, how to put herself on one side, how to give. His dear old face, his dear new face, all hers. He kissed her very hard three times and then he got into the lift and she looked and looked until the door removed him.

That was it, she was on her own, with her wheelie case and tote bag, her knackered old coat. She showed her passport to anyone that cared. She was small, she was loose, she was 100% married. She went through security, which left her where. In the interstitial zone, between Dixons and Ted Baker, a speaker blasting all the old songs, want and love and show me. She'd parked herself by the door to the multi-faith prayer room, people went shuffling by in twos and threes. Her flight was at 2:30, she had three hours, she was already up in the air. She loved him, she loved him. Nick DMed her. How many dreary bepenised bores did they have to blow out of the way to get that decision right, he asked. It hadn't stopped. It would all keep going on and on, with or without her. Kim Jong-un had called Trump a dotard, perhaps they'd all be blown to smithereens. Still, ants at least would proceed, building up their infinite cities, stealing honey from the cupboards. She held on to her bag. She waited for her flight. She loved him, she loved him. Love is the world, pain is the world. She was in it now, she was boarding, there was nowhere to hide.

Something Borrowed

pages

vii 'The cheap 12 inch sq. marble tiles behind speaker at UN always bothered me. I will replace with beautiful large marble slabs if they ask me.': @RealDonaldTrump, Twitter, 3 October 2012.

4 'Wants go so deep there is no way of getting them out of the body': Kathy Acker, *Great Expectations* (Grove Weidenfeld, 1982), p. 127.

6 'more delicate than my cunt': Kathy Acker, postcard to Jonathan Miles, 20 December 1982, in Chris Kraus, *After Kathy Acker* (Allen Lane, 2017), p. 204.

9 'always a john and never a hooker': Zoe Leonard, 'I want a president', 1992.

32 'I'm a totally hideous monster. I'm too ugly to go out into the world': Kathy Acker, *The Adult Life of Toulouse Lautrec* [1975], in *Portrait of an Eye: Three Novels* (Pantheon, 1992), p. 194.

32 'I thought you didn't notice me because I'm so invisible': Kathy Acker, *Translations of the Diaries of Laure the Schoolgirl* [1983], in *Eurydice in the Underworld* (Arcadia, 1997), p. 107.

32 'I'm born poor St Helen's Isle of Wight. 1790. As a child I have hardly any food to eat': Kathy Acker, *The*

135

Childlike Life of the Black Tarantula [1973], in *Portrait of an Eye*, p. 10.

36 'I never saw such terrified people in my life as a group of young men who had run away from Mosul waiting to be vetted by Iraqi security to see if they were former IS fighters. Two men of military age went into a tent for questioning. They were carried to the camp hospital on stretchers two hours later covered in blood.': Patrick Cockburn, 'End Times in Mosul', *London Review of Books*, Vol. 39, No. 17, 17 August 2017, pp. 25–6.

40 'I'm born crazy in the Barbican': Kathy Acker, *The Childlike Life of the Black Tarantula*, in *Portrait of an Eye*, p. 23.

40 'I'm crazy as a bedbug': Kathy Acker, letter to Jackson Mac Low, 7 July 1973, quoted in Chris Kraus, *After Kathy Acker*, p. 82.

40 'I could lead more of my double sexual life in SF etc': Kathy Acker, letter to Jackson Mac Low, July 1973, quoted in Chris Kraus, *After Kathy Acker*, p. 85.

40 'a tree which is the world which is my back': Kathy Acker, *Blood and Guts in High School* (Pan Books, 1984), p. 47.

41 'It was almost an intuitive thing. I was still in the bathroom – in the crime scene. I don't even think I'd stood up. I just typed and typed.': Amber Amour, 'Why I Instagrammed My Rape', *Marie Claire*, 6 June 2016.

42–3 'My first order as President was to renovate and
modernize our nuclear arsenal. It is now far stronger
and more powerful than ever before . . . . . .
Hopefully we will never have to use this power, but
there will never be a time that we are not the most
powerful nation in the world!': @realDonaldTrump,
Twitter, 9 August 2017.

45 'The city panics. Bombers terrorists're going to take
over!': Kathy Acker, *The Adult Life of Toulouse Lautrec*,
in *Portrait of an Eye*, p. 205.

45 'Maybe you're dying and you don't care anymore. You
don't have anything more to say. In the nothingness,
the gray, islands almost disappear into the water.':
Kathy Acker, *Florida*, in *Literal Madness* (Grove Press,
1987), p. 397.

50 'the flesh on the back of his hands was loose like
pieces of wet newspaper'
'most of the dead bodies lay on their stomachs and
were naked scorched black'
'round black balls lay in the sand'
'a child tried to get milk out of her dead mother's
breasts':
Kathy Acker, *My Death My Life By Paolo Pasolini*
[1984], in *Literal Madness*, p. 315.

50 'the only thing I want is all-out war': Kathy Acker,
ibid., p. 233.

53 'disgusting putrid horror-face': Kathy Acker, *Kathy
Goes to Haiti* [1978], in *Literal Madness*, p. 86.

137

54 'Let's communicate w/out hate in our hearts':
@FLOTUS, Twitter, 12 August 2017.

54–5 'The Holocaust was said to have happened in the 40s,
when information was exactly six million times harder
to come by than today. Also, all of the "evidence" was
sealed behind the iron curtain, so no one could even
investigate the sites where it was supposed to have
happened until the 90s': Andrew Anglin, Daily
Stormer, 12 August 2017.

55 'evidence that any more than a few people died
of starvation and disease in these work camps':
Andrew Anglin, Daily Stormer, 12 August 2017.

62 'Here's something you need to know: Caches of
weapons were found throughout Rwanda after the
genocide. This wasn't about the CSA statue, but a test
run for a militia takeover of a small city. I am sorry to
bring you this tonight. There's a bigger plan at work
here. Please don't doubt that. Take nothing for
granted': @kristinrawls, Twitter, 16 August 2017.

69 'Perhaps we need a monument that lists the names of
every enslaved person we can identify, in the tradition
of the Vietnam War memorial': @sarahschulman3,
Twitter, 19 August 2017.

73–4 'Three quarters of these bums're black or Puerto
Rican. The concrete stinks of piss much more than
the surrounding streets smell.': Kathy Acker, *Bodies
of Work* (Serpent's Tail, 1997), p. 107.

74 'how did America begin. To defeat America she had
    to learn who America is'
    'a minor factor in nature, no longer existed'
    'what are the myths of the beginning of America'
    'the desire for religious intolerance made America or
    Freedom':
    Kathy Acker, *Don Quixote* (Paladin, 1986), p. 117.

77 'I stood next to the dummies that are supposed to
    represent black people in their deepest ignominy
    and noticed that there were no dummies that were
    supposed to represent the masters or the mistresses
    of the plantation': Rachel Kaadzi Ghansah, 'A Most
    American Terrorist: The Making of Dylann Roof',
    GQ, 21 August 2017.

78–9 'the very 8½" x 11" multi-use acid-free paper on
    which the workplace discourse is pitilessly inscribed':
    Lucy Ives, 'Sodom, LLC: The Marquis de Sade and
    the Office Novel', *Lapham's Quarterly*, Vol. IX, No. 4,
    Fall 2016.

88 'HISTORIC rainfall in Houston, and all over Texas.
    Floods are unprecedented, and more rain coming.
    Spirit of the people is incredible. Thanks! I will also
    be going to a wonderful state, Missouri, that I won
    by a lot in '16. Dem C.M. is opposed to big tax cuts.
    Republican will win S!': @realDonaldTrump, Twitter,
    27 August 2017.

99 'Knowing is tenuous as a swamp'
    'I'm in the middle of dirt'

'The bodies are thrown in the water'
'I'm with a girlfriend in a real building'
'I want to do more than just see'
'The more flights, the more forgotten':
Kathy Acker, *Eurydice in the Underworld*, p. 15.

100 'A murky yellow liquid that mimics the effect of
heroin. But addicts pay dearly for krokodil's cheap
high. Wherever on the body a user injects the drug,
blood vessels burst and surrounding tissue dies,
sometimes falling off the bone in chunks': Simon
Shuster, 'The World's Deadliest Drug: Inside a
Krokodil Cookhouse', *Time*, 5 December 2013.

109 'they found I could read and they dragged me out to
the barn and gouged my eyes before they beat me':
Jesmyn Ward, *Sing, Unburied, Sing* (Bloomsbury, 2017),
p. 282.

110 'Its walls were painted with manure, I was the only
human here': Dodie Bellamy, *Pink Steam* (Suspect
Thoughts Press, 2004), p. 137.

125 'I never know how to say goodbye. We never do,
do we? Just say "Goodbye."': Kathy Acker, *Blood
and Guts in High School*, p. 31.

125 'I gave the old guy a dirty look':
'I'm not fucking you, I'm your enemy':
Kathy Acker, *Florida*, in *Literal Madness*, p. 401.

125 'I know my grandmother hates my father': Kathy
Acker, *Great Expectations*, p. 14.

125 'I love mommy. I know she's on Dex': Kathy Acker, *Great Expectations*, p. 15.

125 'I didn't feel frightened yet': Kathy Acker, *Florida*, in *Literal Madness*, p. 400.

125 'I myself never commit murder, I'm constantly drunk, I never despair': Kathy Acker, *The Childlike Life of the Black Tarantula*, in *Portrait of an Eye*, pp. 25–7.

125 'I'm as normal as any moral person': Kathy Acker, *Pussy, King of the Pirates* (Grove Press, 1996), p. 84.

125 'As soon as I was clean, again I started haunting clothes stores': Kathy Acker, *Pussy, King of the Pirates*, p. 88.

125 'I grew up wild, I want to stay wild': Kathy Acker, *Blood and Guts in High School*, p. 97.

125 'I felt very happy when my sister's huge hat, while we were both in an auto, flew away': Kathy Acker, *Empire of the Senseless* (Picador, 1988), p. 30.

125–6 'I who would have and would be a pirate: I cannot. I who live in my mind which is my imagination as everything – wanderer adventurer fighter Commander-in-Chief of Allied Forces – I am nothing in these times': Kathy Acker, *Empire of the Senseless*, p. 26.

133 'pain is the world': Kathy Acker, *Blood and Guts in High School*, p. 125.

Thank You

Rebecca Carter & PJ Mark, dream agents

Everyone at Picador, especially Paul Baggaley, Kish Widyaratna and Paul Martinovic

Everyone at Norton, especially Jill Bialosky, Drew Weitman and Erin Lovett

Early readers: Joseph Keckler, Kitty Laing, David Adjmi, Jean Hannah Edelstein, Sarah Wood, Ali Smith, Elizabeth Day, Jon Day, Chantal Joffe, Rich Dodwell, Charlie Porter, Lauren Kassell, David Dernie, Tom de Grunwald, Matt Wolf, Jenny Lord, Francesca Segal

Wolfgang Tillmans and Maureen Paley <3

Chris Kraus, for planting the seed; Kathy Acker, for making such radical possibilities; Matias Viegener, for your generosity

Denise Laing, always

& Ian Patterson, for everything